Strebor on the Streetz

Gutta MAMIS

ALSO BY N'TYSE

Twisted Seduction

Twisted Vows of Seduction

Strebor on the Streetz

MAMIS

EDITED BY

N'TYSE

C.J. HUDSON, KAI, BRANDIE DAVIS

FOREWORD BY ANNA J

SBI

STREBOR BOOKS

NEW YORK LONDON TORONTO SYDNEY

Strebor Books
P.O. Box 6505
Largo, MD 20792
http://www.streborbooks.com

This book is a work of fiction. Names, characters, places and incidents are products of the author's imagination or are used fictitiously. Any resemblance to actual events or locales or persons, living or dead, is entirely coincidental.

ISBN 978-1-59309-524-6
ISBN 978-1-4767-4450-6 (ebook)
LCCN 2014931193

First Strebor Books trade paperback edition August 2014

Cover design: www.mariondesigns.com
Cover photograph: © Keith Saunders/Keith Saunders Photos

10 9 8 7 6 5 4 3 2 1

Manufactured in the United States of America

For information regarding special discounts for bulk purchases, please contact Simon & Schuster Special Sales at 1-866-506-1949 or business@simonandschuster.com

The Simon & Schuster Speakers Bureau can bring authors to your live event. For more information or to book an event, contact the Simon & Schuster Speakers Bureau at 1-866-248-3049 or visit our website at www.simonspeakers.com.

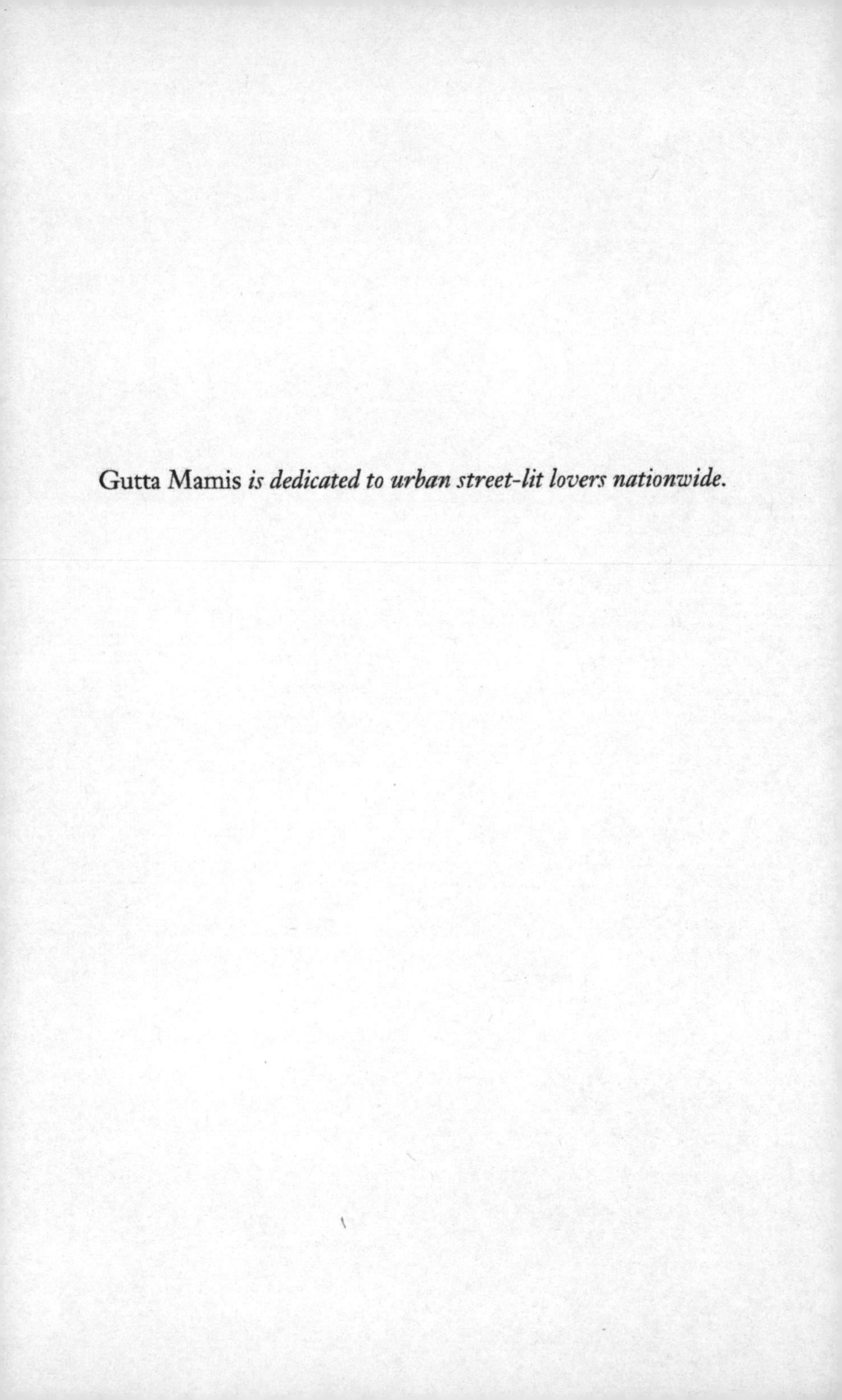

Gutta Mamis *is dedicated to urban street-lit lovers nationwide.*

ACKNOWLEDGMENTS

As always, thanks to those who have supported my every endeavor; my loving and supportive family, friends, author peers, Rockstar writers in the Facebook Strebor group, and readers near and far. Much gratitude to Zane who has been more than just my publisher, but my mentor. I'm honored to be under your tutelage. Charmaine, you are absolutely the greatest! It's always a pleasure to work with you on my projects. A gazillion thanks to all of the bookclubs, bookstores, online reading groups, Black Expressions, magazines, and distributors who made this project possible by providing urban fiction authors an outlet to expose their work. Lastly, thanks to the talented contributors of this project: Kai, C.J. Hudson, and Brandie Davis. You guys rock!

TABLE OF CONTENTS

xi *Foreword* Anna J

1 *Twisted Loyalty* Kai

61 *Three the Hard Way* C.J. Hudson

125 *The Face of Death* Brandie Davis

187 *Chasers* N'TYSE

FOREWORD

It's only natural for a man to run the spot; that's the way of human nature. For years the man went out and brought home the bacon, and the woman's job was to fry it up. Well, the tables have turned and now it's time for folks to recognize who's really the boss. Women are born with a survival instinct. It's do or die, or nothing at all. And just like a pit bull, when she gets a taste for blood, she won't stop until the fight is truly over. A woman scorned is one to watch out for, and she will protect what is hers or die trying.

What happens when the code of the streets is broken? There's no room for a seven-day bleeding chick to sit on top, or is there? The game is about to change and these Gutta Mamis are making all the rules. It has been said that when a woman is in charge, everything runs smoothly, but when loyalty is tested and no one wants to answer to a woman, it's time for the guns to come out. The same person that can be as soft and sweet as a butterfly can wreak havoc on the whole crew in a blink of the eye and you'll never know what hit you. A freak in the sheets, and a bulldozer everywhere else. You ain't ready.

The crème de la crème of street lit have been called to bring you the real deal. By the time you finish "Twisted Loyalty" by Kai, "Three the Hard Way" by C.J. Hudson, "The Face of Death" by Brandie Davis, and "Chasers" by the supreme queen herself, N'Tyse, you'll look at women in a whole new light. So if I were you, I'd find a nice comfortable seat; you'll be here for a while. Now sit back, and enjoy the ride.

Anna J

Twisted LOYALTY

BY KAI

1

The taste of death always made Tandra nervous. It was an automatic reaction—when the scent wafted under her nose, her hands trembled and her mind scrambled. And death had a taste, just like a horrific fart in a tight, enclosed space. It burned the nose and somehow clawed at the taste buds, making Tandra's gag reflex tear at her empty stomach. She hated death, but she relied on death. She profited from death. Tandra needed death to survive.

It was the flaw of being a Cleaner; the ramification of facing life's feces on a weekly basis. It wasn't worth it—wasn't worth scrubbing herself until her skin peeled raw, trying to remove all DNA and accidental evidence. Wasn't worth the blank dreams, nights of black voids behind closed eyelids, showing her soul's destination was nothing more than a vast black hole.

Being a Cleaner had cost her everything. But the painful price was internal. Externally, Tandra was the shit. She was the best Cleaner in the city—the only professional Cleaner left. There were others on the come-up, but the top dogs used her. Seth, her mentor, had retired as soon as she was old enough to handle the connections. He had placed his business in her hands. Only the elite knew of her, only the top crime scenes needed her, and very, very few could afford her. When she came in, the scene was *cleaned*—no matter how contaminated it had been. Her reputation was all she had and it was contingent on her clients walking away clean from any charges; no links to the scene. Ever.

Tandra swallowed. The scent of death had overwhelmed her when she and Lenora stepped into the small apartment. The call had come a few hours after the damage had been done—the time it had taken for the fools to report their own stupidity to their boss, to admit that unchecked emotions or a chemical-induced high had caused them to murder an apartment full of people and leave a homicide detective's wet dream in their wake.

If the call hadn't come directly from Crown, Tandra wouldn't have answered it. Shit, Tandra still shouldn't have answered. She observed the mess in front of her with disgust. Crown's people were taking her services for granted, getting messier and messier with their shit by the job. She and Crown were going to have a talk; that much was fucking evident. It was a talk that she dreaded, but at the same time, it couldn't be avoided. Murder was a grueling enough business, sloppiness was an unnecessary detraction, and for the waste of her damn time to take the extra cleaning steps necessary, she was going to charge Crown much, much more.

"Watchu think?" Lenora stood next to Tandra, her little sister in spirit. "Is it worth it?"

Tandra glanced at Lenora. It was a stupid question. "What is there to think?" Tandra lowered her eyes and finally acknowledged the dead body at her toes. "We're here now. Ain't no walking away."

"True." Lenora shrugged.

Tandra moved her foot until the dead man's cheekbone rested at the tip of her slanted stiletto boots. The boots were a necessity on these jobs. During job entry and observation, they kept her step light and narrow. More importantly, the smooth bottom with silicone covering left no shoe imprint in the blood on the floor.

The dead man was handsome, even in the early hours of death. That was rare to observe. Tandra pushed him with her toe, pressed in his cheek with the sharp tip point of her stiletto. He looked familiar, but she couldn't place the face—not at the moment. Too bad he was dead. Tandra imagined that he might have been worth testing out. But he had crossed Crown or tangled with Crown's people, either directly or vicariously. He should have known that death would be the price.

"Stupid bastard," Tandra snorted as she stepped over him. Her nerves were resetting themselves like they always did within minutes of her observing a scene. She refused to let her weakness show, not even to Lenora, whom she trusted with her life. This game was just like any other, filled with people trying to gain access through illegal means. Weakness could never be exposed, not even to Lenora.

"Let's get to it, then." Lenora turned away from her and stepped gingerly back to the front door where they had placed their supplies.

"How much time?" Tandra stepped over another body and took three more steps to the center of the room. She always counted her steps, always knew just how quickly she could enter or exit any space. It was a necessary practice in this line of work.

"Long enough." Lenora bent over to touch her toes, stretching out her long thin body in the tight-fitting bodysuit that clung to her like a second skin. "What did Detrick say?"

"Detrick is an asshole. What would he know?" Tandra surveyed the dingy room.

Detrick was the connection to Crown whom Tandra normally went through. At first, Tandra had thought the job was a set-up. She could never be sure, never know who was next to try to replace her. Until a few hours ago, she had never heard Crown's voice. When the proper English accent filled her Bluetooth, the voice calm, cold and exact, Tandra thought for a second that her time had finally come. She lived every day knowing that it was around the corner. When Crown had laid out the job details, Tandra knew it was for real. She had to cut him off midsentence; she didn't discuss business over the phone. While she was below the radar, Crown definitely wasn't, and Tandra wasn't going to risk taking on heat talking on a tapped line. Instead, Tandra had arranged for the details to be delivered to her by one of Crown's nobodies. Crown's guidelines were very specific, although they were rules Tandra followed, anyway: No evidence; no discussion of any kind with anyone about the job; and Tandra was to meet directly with Crown upon completion.

But Detrick should have made the call to Tandra, not Crown, and the fact that he didn't made Tandra uncomfortable. For now, she didn't trust anything related to this job.

"Why you got to call Detrick an asshole, Tandy, damn." Lenora shrugged. "He's never been wrong before."

Tandra didn't answer. She didn't fill her employees in on the details, whether she loved them or not.

Blood was splashed against the wallpaper and pooled next to another body that sat propped in the corner. The curtains against the picture window were torn and shabby, and also covered with blood. Food sat half-eaten on the dining room table. "It's gonna be a full job. We will need at least five hours." Tandra glanced along the bottom of the curtain, looking for evidence of another body.

"Be safe; do it in less than three."

"Bullshit." Tandra took eight steps to the window—another body lay beneath the windowsill. "Impossible."

Lenora shrugged. "Got to try, Tandy. It's best to be safe, anyway. We got to be out of here before sunrise."

"Let Detrick know we are charging double—no less than forty for this job."

"Forty g's?"

"No doubt."

"If you say so, mamacita." Lenora continued removing the squares of folded plastic that they normally used to cover furniture while they painted.

Tandra glanced over her shoulder. "You might as well save those. The furniture has to go."

Lenora looked at the mess around them. "You're right."

Tandra counted fourteen steps to the bathroom and glanced in. "All the walls have to be painted. Gonna have to call in Breeze." The bathroom was empty. Relieved, she took nine more steps to the small bedroom in the back.

"Gotdamn, I don't want to deal with Breeze's ass tonight. She always got some smart shit to say. I don't want to hear nothing about her, her women or her damn dildos."

Tandra laughed, a quiet chuckle. She moved silently into the bedroom, careful not to touch the walls or any of the furniture. Blood was everywhere. She had on the same black bodysuit that Lenora wore. Its tight fit came in handy, minimized the risk of her touching anything or leaving fabric residue of any kind. A man lay with his throat slit against the open closet door. "How much acetone did we bring?"

"A gallon," Lenora softly called.

Another body lay at the foot of the bed, a bullet hole through his forehead. This was the largest job Tandra had been given. "Tell Breeze we need more acetone, more *Burner*, more paint, more paint thinner. She gonna have to bring the van, too. Black drop-cloths for the windows. Ten of them. Tacks. Two more boxes of garbage bags. One box of Ziploc gallon bags. Two fluorescent flashlights—there's gonna be a million prints up in here and we got to get them all. A Shop-Vac. Tell her a new one is in the back of the warehouse, by the shelves." Burner was the special mix of chemicals that Seth had created years ago, which ate away flesh and weakened bone. Tandra mixed it—she was the only other person who knew the formula.

"Anything else, ma?"

"Tell her ass to open and put the Shop-Vac together *before* she gets here." Dealing with Breeze, the instructions had to be detailed. "I don't want no big-ass boxes left in the Dumpster here."

"No doubt."

Tandra never had to worry about Lenora forgetting anything. Her mind was like a tape recorder—another reason that Tandra never said anything to her that might be sensitive. Lenora stored everything in that computer brain of hers.

Tandra listened as Lenora spoke softly into the phone, placing the call to Breeze on the disposable cell phone. Text messages were out; anything written was forbidden. The phones had been purchased and distributed that morning, a weekly routine among Tandra's employees. She was careful with her people, with their careers, with their lives.

As careful as she could be.

Tandra observed the lumpy, king-size bed. It was pushed against the far wall; its footboard faced the door. Tandra clicked her tongue. "These folks obviously don't know a damn thing about feng shui."

"Huh?"

"Feng shui. They got the feet of the bed facing the door."

Lenora laughed. "Here you go with your karma shit. Feet can't face the door, because…?"

"You surely don't listen—I told you this before. The dead are carried out feet first. So you don't sleep in that position with your feet toward the door. Horrible for your energy and alignment."

"Tandy, I am sure the idiot who lived here ain't thinking about that right now. He's trying to get his soul into heaven, no doubt."

"No doubt," Tandra whispered as she approached the bed. Either her eyes were playing tricks on her, or the end of the sheet, on the other side of the bed had moved. The movement was slight, like the tickle of a breeze. But there was no breeze in this cold-ass apartment.

"Lenora..."

"Tandy, I already called Breeze. Don't start fussing, with your impatient ass. She was already on her way, but she is going to stop by the warehouse."

"Lenora, come here." Tandra tried to keep her voice calm. Her steady eyes counted four more steps between the dresser and the bed.

Tandra could hear Lenora moving quickly as she changed for the gruesome task ahead. "I am not about to call Detrick. You the one always pressing me about not using a cell on the job. Always worried about our location being tracked. So I damn sure ain't calling Detrick on his for real cell from this spot."

The sheet moved again; it lifted just a hair of an inch. Tandra snatched the Beretta that was strapped to the leather band around her thigh. She aimed at the sheet. The lump wasn't undefined anymore. Now Tandra made out the outline of a person, lying among the bundled mess, under the sheets.

Asleep?

Fear hadn't etched its way into her mind yet. She didn't know what to expect, but her first instinct of shoot first, question later, hadn't taken over yet. Tandra trained her gun on the bed as she slowly backtracked to the bedroom door; her eyes locked on the bed. "Nora."

Lenora stopped talking. Their eyes met. Lenora tilted her head, questioning. Tandra nodded forward to the room, confirming. Lenora snatched off her wig, threw it in the box in front of her, and trotted quickly to the other side of the doorframe as she snatched the Glocks that were strapped to either of her thighs.

The two women waited in thick silence. Seconds clicked by. Tandra nodded her head at Lenora, who stepped back into the room. Tandra followed. Both ladies had the bed covered, three fully loaded barrels ready to rain hell down upon whatever lay beneath the sheet. They stood on either side of the bed. Lenora took careful aim at center mass. Tandra yanked at the blanket and sheet from the foot of the bed. The mess tumbled to the side.

Handcuffed to the side of the bed frame was a young woman; blood was splattered across her forehead, smeared on her chin and sprinkled across her naked body.

The victim's wide eyes blinked with fear.

"Shit—," Tandra whispered.

"—she's alive," Lenora said, completing Tandra's thought and speaking aloud their worst fear.

2

"This is unfucking believable." Lenora dropped both her guns at her sides. "How is she alive?"

Tandra didn't answer, her mind was reeling. A witness. She had never had a witness before. She had said Lenora's name out loud, called out Breeze, had responded to the name "Tandy." The woman's eyes were locked on Lenora's guns right now, taking in the slope of the narrow barrels against Lenora's manicured fingers. Their cover was compromised.

"Tandy, what the fuck?"

Tandra shook her head. There was nothing to discuss. The answer was clear and obvious.

Lenora took a step closer to the woman. The woman's breathing increased; she whimpered and shrunk into a tight ball. The dead bastards around them, or the filth that worked for Crown, had ravaged her; that much was obvious. "What the hell did these motherfuckers do to you?"

The woman opened her mouth to speak. "Please ..." Her thin frame trembled.

"What happened?"

"Nora, stop asking her questions." Tandra took a step back. She was trying to piece together the mess in front of her.

"Naw, this don't make no damn sense. Watchu do that got you tied up in this shit, ma?"

Tandra glanced at the woman's hands. Both were empty. Tandra's eyes traveled up her wrists to the woman's arms. The track marks along her light-brown skin were unmistakable.

The girl squinted at them. She focused on Tandra as Lenora took a step closer, her mouth open.

"What the fuck?" Lenora tapped the side of her thigh with one of the Glocks, a nervous habit.

Tandra immediately noticed it. "Calm the fuck down, Nora, before you shoot your damn self."

Lenora looked at her with a blank expression, fear flooded her eyes.

"Look at me, Nora. Calm down. Breathe." Tandra glanced at the woman's long, black, tousled weave, which clung to her face and neck. She noticed the woman wasn't offering up any information or explanation, wasn't crying or screaming or asking to be released. Either she was in shock, or she was deeply involved in what had gone down.

"Shit." Lenora took a step back. They hadn't seen this before, hadn't ever walked up on some type of weird rape scene where the victim was still alive in the middle of dead bodies. "What the hell happened?"

Tears finally poured down the girl's face, mixing with the already smeared mascara and blood. "Oh, thank God. I thought y'all was going to do more. I thought y'all was with them."

"Nora, don't ask this bitch shit." Tandra's voice was low, barely audible. "For all we know, she's a part of this mess for a reason. Or she here to do us."

"What?" Lenora's innocent eyes reminded Tandra of her youngest son's. Deer eyes. "Look at her, Tandy." Lenora moved a step closer to the bed. "And why would anyone want to do us?"

"Nora..."

"I can't move my arm; it's numb." The woman twisted in anguish. "Please let me loose."

Lenora raised her gun to shoot at the cuffs.

"Hell no," Tandra's sharp voice tore through the room. "Nora, she could have cuffed herself. Think about it. Don't touch her."

"Please," the woman shouted, "you can't leave me like this. I was hiding cuz I thought y'all was them."

"Who is them? Who did this?" Lenora stooped lower, closer to the woman.

Tandra's gut twisted violently. Something was dead ass wrong about this. "Back the fuck up, Nora."

The woman's free hand slid under the pillow lying near her waist. Nora didn't notice; her eyes were locked on Tandra in confusion. Tandra's eyes widened in panic, her worst nightmare was taking place right before her eyes.

"Noo!" The scream ripped from her essence as Tandra fired her Beretta. The silencer minimized the explosion down to a dull, slapping sound.

It took Nora a moment before she realized what was happening. In her surprise, she fell backward, knocking her head against the dresser as she ducked.

Tandra's bullets pelted the woman in her mouth, forehead and throat.

Then there was nothing but silence.

Tandra's heart beat so fast she thought it was going to explode. She was a Cleaner, not a damn murderer. *Shit!*

"Gotdamn, Tandy, what the fuck did you just do?"

"That bitch was moving for a gun." Tandra's fury was thick. "I told you to move back from her. Fuck. Why the fuck did you get so close to her?"

"You ain't have to kill her. She ain't been through enough?"

Lenora stepped back from the body, still clenching her guns, one hand over her mouth, the other at her waist. "Look at her body, Tandra. Look at what the fuck they did to her."

"She's a fucking fiend, Nora." Tandra pointed her finger at the woman's arms. "You can't trust shit a fiend say or do. You think I'ma put me or you at risk over a fiend?"

"But Tandra—"

"Fuck that. She was a plant, Nora. Read it—look at the scene for what it is. An apartment full of dead folks, but she up in here alive? Ain't nobody in here with their pants off, they shirts off—who was fucking her when they got killed? No damn body. She was a plant, Lenora."

Lenora stood quiet for a few minutes, her hands shaking. "What does that mean, Tandra?"

"It means that this scene might be a setup. I could have been a target. We could have been the targets."

"Or, she could have been a victim that happened to survive." Lenora stepped away from the bed. "Why isn't that an option?"

"Then what was she reaching for under the pillow?"

Lenora shrugged.

Tandy yanked the pillow off the tattered sheets and threw it on the floor. A sharp blade lay on the mattress.

"That don't make no fucking sense." Lenora stomped back to the main room. "What the fuck was she going to do with a knife?"

"Hell if I know. But I wasn't waiting to see."

"Do we finish the job, or run for our lives, Miss Paranoid?"

Tandra sighed. She was half a heartbeat away from cussing Lenora out. "Drop the sarcastic bullshit. We finish the job, cuz we don't know for sure. And cuz your stupid ass bumped all into the dresser and your DNA is up in here, now."

The front door opened. Both Tandra and Lenora trained their guns at the door. Tandra was ready to kill anyone who moved wrong.

"What's up, hoes?" Breeze's broad body filled the doorway, rolling a huge black suitcase full of supplies. The suitcase matched Tandra's and Lenora's.

Tandra breathed. "Anybody see you?"

"Who you asking—what the hell you think?" Breeze snorted, then glanced at Lenora and winked. "What's up, Scrawny?"

"Not now, Breeze." Lenora shook her head. "I don't have patience for your shit tonight."

"Daaamn, what the fuck is up with you two?" No one bothered to answer her. Breeze surveyed the room. "Someone got it in up in here—gotdamn!"

More silence as Tandra stared toward the bedroom and Lenora fidgeted near the supplies.

"Hello?" Breeze clapped her broad hands together; her gray eyes sparkled. She wore her hair in a short soft fro, having cut her long locs once she became a full-time Cleaner. Her broad frame was tone, she kept her body fit—but she refused to wear the tight-fitted cat suit, which didn't fit her demeanor at all. Black hoodie over a black, fitted T-shirt, resting on top of black jeans neatly laid on and black Nikes were her preferred uniform. "Y'all ain't did shit up in here. Damn. Talk about wasting time—y'all been here for damn near half an hour, right?"

No answer.

Breeze pulled at the black wristband she wore, which covered her tattoo. "Somebody gonna answer me, I know that much."

Breeze stepped into the bathroom. "At least one room is clean." She hedged around toward the bedroom. "Three more bodies in here? Whose set is this?"

"Crown's."

"For real?" Breeze shook her head. "Who is this bitch on the bed...oh shit!"

"What?" Tandra started unloading supplies and placing them around the room for Lenora and Breeze, to limit the time of moving back and forth. "Lenora, get to work."

Tandra's tone was rude on purpose; it was time to reset order, get the job done, and get the fuck out of dodge. She would have to analyze this shit later.

Breeze stepped back in the main room. "Crown done sent us to a hot spot for real. Y'all know who that chick is on the bed?"

Lenora shook her head. "I was trying to find out when—"

"Nora, shut the fuck up!" Tandra spun around. "What the fuck is wrong with you? You can't keep shit to yourself...you don't know the field you in? I swear to God—" Tandra dropped the paint she was carrying; Breeze jumped and caught it before it rolled.

Breeze interjected. "Damnit, Tandra, the point is to not be seen. You think neighbors ain't gonna hear paint cans dropping and rolling across the damn floor?"

Tandra ignored Breeze, still shouting at Lenora. "—open your fucking mouth about it again, Nora, and it's you and me. For real."

Lenora didn't look up.

Tandra's deep brown skin seemed to turn black with anger.

Breeze quietly put the paint can down, assessing the situation around her. She hadn't made it from hustling to cleaning to being a successful business owner based on stupidity. She met eyes with Tandra, and sent her a steady calm look of warning. It was a reminder: They needed Lenora to get through the job. Lenora was young and inexperienced. And, if she had to be handled, she could be dealt with later. Breeze knew that they couldn't afford to have the job fall apart right now, not during the middle of it, not with the discovery she had just made, not with the amount of bodies that had to be eliminated.

Tandra held Breeze's gaze. She bit her lip and breathed quietly.

Lenora blinked back tears of anger as she stared at the floor. Tandra realized it might have been the first time Lenora had seen Tandra kill someone in cold blood. It was different, to kill a person like that, someone Lenora already believed was a victim and who had just survived hell. But, Tandra didn't know the fiend to give a fuck about her. Lenora was her responsibility, so was Breeze, and wasn't none of them getting twisted up in someone else's bullshit.

Nora wiped at her eyes with the back of her hand.

Tandra strapped her gun back on her thigh. She had been holding it without realizing it. "C'mon. Let's get this shit over with."

"Tandra, I'ma start in the bedroom." Breeze headed to the room.

Tandra took the hint and followed her. "Whatsup?"

"I don't know what the fuck is going on here, but this bitch here work for Detrick."

"What?"

"I know her; she a stripper down at Mira's spot. PJ, that's her name. But she work for Detrick; set niggas up for him—"

Tandra squinted. "You thinking…"

"I don't know. But no way would Detrick kill his own bitch. They been tight for years. He called us in on this scene?"

Tandra shook her head "no." "Crown did."

"Well, maybe him or Detrick set someone up and it went wrong. That's probably what it is. They must have figured out the setup and killed her before they got got. You should just know…just be aware. It's gonna be some serious bloodshed around this. Detrick got kids by her."

Tandra glanced back at Lenora. Breeze was her full partner, the one person who could handle business as efficiently as herself. "B, she was alive when we got here."

"Huh?"

Tandra looked into Breeze's eyes.

"What you saying?"

There was no way Tandra was going to say it out loud. She glanced down at her Beretta. Breeze followed her eyes, took in the Beretta against her thick thigh and then looked at the dead woman in the bed.

The question in Breeze's eyes forced Tandra to respond.

"She went for the knife."

Breeze's mouth dropped open, but she quickly recovered. "I heard that's her skill. She got a thing for knives."

"I bet."

"Let's get the job done and get the fuck outta here. We'll figure this out later."

3

Four hours later, the three Cleaners prepared to depart from the scene, exhaustion seeping into their bones like arthritis. Tandra had the bullet remnants in neat Ziploc bags; she would dispose of them like she always did. Breeze walked away with the bone fragments that the Burner hadn't been able to eat through; she was responsible for their final resting place. Lenora was too new to the game to walk away with evidence of any type. She hadn't risen to that status and, after tonight, the chances that she could be trusted like that were decreasing.

Talking was at a minimum anyway during these jobs, between the painting and disposing. But tonight, Tandra had kept her mouth locked and her ears open for any sign of sabotage. She could just be paranoid. She probably was. But this job felt different, like dipping her feet into a pond of grease, leaving a nasty trail wherever she went. Tandra knew that tonight wouldn't just disappear into her memories, leaving her clients with further evidence of her excellent professionalism and a bountiful payday. Nope, tonight would be one she would have to answer for, as sure as the night was long, because tonight she had taken a life. In the name of Cleaning. A life that was connected to her main contact. There was no way this situation was happenstance, no way it wouldn't stain her in some way.

"I'm out." Breeze pulled a baseball cap low over her eyes, and threw her hoodie on over it. Tandra noticed her eyes were glassed over. It had to be stress, Breeze never got tired during a job.

Tandra nodded. She and Breeze exchanged a pregnant pause; Breeze glanced at Lenora. Lenora remained silent, tugging back on the wig that she had snatched off earlier.

"You good, Chicken Bones?"

"Fuck you, Breeze." Lenora's voice was quiet and unsteady.

"Yeah, you gonna be all right." Breeze smiled. "It's the job. You understand that, right?"

Tandra kept her head down. Breeze was testing Lenora out, trying to figure out how she was going to play it. Obviously, Lenora didn't realize it.

Tandra held her breath and prayed that Lenora would woman up. Breeze wasn't like Tandra and Lenora—dropping someone who put Breeze or her enterprise at risk was nothing but the cost of doing business to her. Lenora could be the next body wrapped in plastic and dragged to the tub if she didn't play it right. Tandra could tell by Breeze's stance, her rigid shoulders and the slight slant of her head that Lenora's very existence was on the line.

Lenora sighed and finished zipping her suitcase. "Yeah, Breeze, I know. It just shook me up for a sec." She stood up straight. "Everyone ain't like your gangsta ass, all right? Somc of us ain't seen a person get killed right in front of us." Lenora looked at both of them. "Y'all can understand that, can't you? I ain't never seen no shit like that before."

Tandra nodded. She didn't feel any better.

Breeze's shoulders lowered a little bit and her hand moved from her hip, where she kept her 45mm. "Yeah, Scrawny, I see you."

"Tired of your damn nicknames, bitch; I look good." Lenora laughed.

"Aw shit." That brought a smile out of Breeze. She looked back at Tandra. "Hit me later."

"No doubt."

Breeze eased out of the apartment and disappeared down the hall. A few minutes later, Lenora followed; at the end of the hall, she walked in the opposite direction than Breeze had taken. Tandra was always the last to leave the scene. She shut the door with gloved hands and headed for the exit.

Tandra went through the motions without thinking. She needed a release, a way to free her mind from the doom that hounded her. Tandra pulled into the tiny apartment that she went to immediately after jobs. She never entered her real home, where her children resided, with death's residue on her. That was a no-no. In the small efficiency apartment, Tandra keyed in the alarm code and then eyed the space to make sure it was just as she left it. Satisfied, she stripped off her wig, the gloves, her boots and the jumpsuit. All of it went into another Ziploc bag for disposal. Naked, Tandra glanced around the empty space. It was too quiet; her thoughts were able to find their way to the forefront of her mind.

Tandra clicked on the iPod that lay on the small night table next to the bed. Hezekiah Walker's "Praise Him In Advance" filled the room. Tandra stood still. The last thing she wanted to listen to was gospel music. The last thing she wanted to think about was being a murderer in the eyes of God.

Tandra clicked the small pad until "Get Down" from the Clipse filled the room. That was better. She could ride the vibes of the mellow flow and let the beat move her body without thought.

"Trust, I know them twenties real well." Tandra whispered the lyrics as she finally climbed into the shower and turned the dial as hot as it would go. She gritted her teeth and stood under the thick blast of hot water, forcing herself to cope with the burning sensation pelting her body. Tandra scrubbed every inch of her body as tears rolled down her face. She ignored the torture that she was putting herself through; she deserved the pain. It reminded her that she was weak, human and flawed. There couldn't be any trace of that awful place left on her body; no hint of what she had done could be on her person. All of it, the stench of death, the cleansing of filth and the life she had taken, had to swirl down the drain with the hot water and the soap suds. This was where she would leave it, in the shower stall.

Tandra finally climbed out of the shower. The cold air stung her raw skin. She methodically patted herself dry and applied a thin layer of Vaseline to her body. Her cell rang.

"Yeah."

"Hey, babe, you hit me?"

Lyell. He was just the person Tandra wanted to hear; the one man who filled her empty spaces without question or obligation. "Yes, I did."

"What's up?"

"I need you." She had no room for bullshit tonight; no filters to block out the simple longing that invaded her. It was a welcome distraction.

"Damn, shorty, you are a trip."

"Whatever."

He paused. "What's wrong?"

"Nothing." Tandra damn sure wasn't going to discuss tonight with him or anybody else. No one knew what she did. To the world, she was the owner of a successful salon and any work-related stress was in handling the mountain of stylists and specialists who all had egos as large as an elephant's ass, but varied in work ethic; normally the biggest pain in the ass was the least dependable and the loudest fight. "The usual."

"Want me to come to you?"

That's why she more than liked Lyell; he was considerate and kind. Very patient. And very private. A rare find.

"No." No one knew about the efficiency apartment either. Tandra was juggling life like a three-ring circus. "Can I come over?"

"Always." Lyell chuckled. "I'll be waiting."

4

"Why are you shaking?" Detrick stared down at Lenora like she was an alien. Cocoa brown with pitch-black eyes, Detrick was the finest brother Lenora had ever laid eyes on. But she would never let him know that.

"Because I am cold and tired. Are you going to let me in?" Lenora rocked back on her bowlegs and crossed her arms.

Detrick took the cigar out of his mouth and looked her up and down. "Where you coming from looking like Catwoman?"

"A job, Detrick, damn. Move out of the way." Lenora pushed her way past the door and into Detrick's house.

"Shorty, you got me twisted, just coming over my house unannounced."

"For real?" Lenora started looking around his space and her eyes went to the staircase. "Who the fuck you got over here?"

"Oh, you laying claim to me now?" Detrick laughed; the rich sound bounced off the high ceilings of his home. "What you gonna do if I did have someone over here?"

"You want to try me?" Lenora's hand went to her thighs and her cape fell back.

"Nora, you done came over here strapped? What the fuck?" Detrick plopped on his brown leather sofa, laughing. "What's up with you, Shorty?"

"I'm about to go." Lenora was sick of Detrick already; tired of him always laughing at her. She turned around to leave.

"You ain't going no damn where. Bring your ass back over here."

"Fuck you, Detrick. I had a long-ass night."

Detrick jumped off the couch and chased after her. "Nora..." He grabbed her arm. "Why you got to be on fire like that dere?" he said with a heavy accent for a second, before switching back to his normal jargon. Detrick caught her just as she reached the door. "You know you don't want to leave."

Lenora pushed him back. "I ain't come over here for this shit."

"Well, Cutie, what you here for?"

Lenora closed her eyes and breathed in deeply. She could smell curry chicken in the house. Only Detrick kept Batman hours, eating curry chicken at close to five in the morning. "I'm tired as hell, Detrick."

He pressed his body against hers. Lenora could smell the cigar smoke on his breath and the fragrant scent of weed on his tongue. "You want for me to put you to sleep, eh?"

His scent immediately relaxed her. Lenora put her hands on his chest. "Can you make the nightmares go away?" she whispered.

"You know that I can." Detrick's voice was raspy; his tongue was already on her neck.

"Make them go away, then." Lenora met his eyes.

"I always do." Detrick held her gaze as he pushed against her; her arms stayed at her side. He took a step back and observed her in the body leotard, tracing a finger along her inner thigh to the crown of her pleasure. With his other hand, his finger lightly trailed along her hip, danced along the curve of her belly, slid up her long, narrow torso, and rested on her breast.

Lenora unstrapped her Glocks and laid them on the floor. She closed her eyes. Her mouth fell open. Detrick's hands and the power of his touch were second to none.

He kissed her. The feel of his lips took her breath away.

"Take this thing off." Detrick pulled at her body suit.

Lenora met his eyes and took in his power. She had no choice but to obey and slid it down to her waist.

Detrick's hands covered her breasts and groped them, his thumb lightly teasing her nipples. With each grope, Lenora felt a different sensation down her spine. For a second, she felt off-balance as she leaned in to his firm grip.

Detrick ran his hand down the middle of her back. He tugged the suit past her hips down to her thighs. His fingers followed, pressing against her tingling skin as his tongue traced a path along her neck. "Is this what you came over here for?"

Lenora didn't answer.

Detrick pressed her against the door again, this time picking her up by both her arms. She easily straddled him as she stared into his black eyes. "Tell me," Detrick's strong accent pushed through again. "This be what you want?"

Lenora nodded. Detrick filled his mouth with both her breasts, his tongue flicking across her nipples in an erratic rhythm. She moaned and grabbed his head, her fingers laying against his close-cut hair.

"Say you want it." Detrick's raspy command sprinkled Lenora with delight.

"Give it to me, Daddy."

He sucked on her breast as two fingers inserted between her thighs. "Say you want it."

Lenora closed her eyes; the sensation of his mouth on her breasts and his fingers between her legs overwhelmed her. She couldn't say shit.

"Say it, ma."

"I want it."

"How you want it?" He let go of her and she slid back down to the floor. Detrick put his feet inside of hers and spread her legs open.

"However you give it to me, daddy."

Detrick stopped and stared at her. That was the passcode he rarely received. He looked deep in her eyes to make sure he wasn't hearing things. "You sure, Nora."

Nora knew what she was asking. She was requesting Detrick hit that spot that no other person had ever had access to. The night had been too much; Lenora felt the need to surrender herself completely to someone else's will. Detrick exuded power anyway, but to give him anal access, she had to completely release her mind to him. It was the only way to get past the pain. And once he was completely in her head, the pain was a weird exotic pleasure that tap-danced across every nerve ending up and down her spine until she couldn't take it anymore, until the sensitivity of it almost made her pass out in pleasure. Detrick caused her a different type of orgasm—one that overloaded her brain and caused her to scream in pleasure. "Give it to me, baby. I want you like that."

Detrick didn't wait to hear anything else and he definitely wasn't going to give her a chance to change her mind. He turned her around and pressed her against the door, her breasts pushed against the thick wooden frame.

"Slow, Detrick, go slow."

"I won't hurt you, baby." Detrick slid a condom out of his pocket and tore the wrapper off.

"Hurry up," Lenora whimpered.

Detrick rolled the condom down on his length, then he wrapped his arms around Lenora and again pushed his fingers in the top of her thighs as he bit the back of her neck. "You're so damn sexy." His thick erection lingered on her behind.

She groaned. Detrick was the only one she trusted like this, the only one who she had opened up her mind to like that. She knew deep in her heart that she could trust Detrick; he would never hurt her.

He kissed the back of her neck again. "Are you ready?" He pulled her body away from the door and flush against his own; her curved back was just inches from his chest as her behind rested fully on his pelvis. Detrick grabbed her onion bottom and caressed it, his touch interchanged from a feather stroke to a heavy grope.

"Do it, baby, please."

"Relax." Detrick's voice in her ear was hypnotic; his hands still groped a beautiful rhythm on her breasts and her front inner petals until her wetness covered his hands and seeped back on his centered mass, giving him the lubrication he needed.

Detrick pressed into her tight space. Lenora grunted out loud and called his name, the lust in her voice for this unique craving that she only had with Detrick turned him on more. He spread his legs wider, which spread her legs wider, and pressed her flush against the door again. Lenora turned her head to the side to breathe. Her nails scratched at the door. Detrick kissed her ear, earlobe, the side of her face. Detrick placed his hands flush on the wall as he pressed again, slowly, inch by inch, into Lenora's forbidden space.

"Ow, baby, stop. I can't do it." The pain was always greater than Lenora remembered. "I changed my mind."

"Relax, baby, just relax." Detrick stuck his tongue in her ear. "I won't hurt you." He pushed in a little further.

She groaned louder.

"Do you need me to stop?"

"No, baby," Lenora grunted, her breathing heavy. "Don't listen to me. Don't stop."

He pushed again, going deeper. She screamed and in that second, pleasure replaced pain, as she clawed at the wall. "Right there, baby," Lenora gasped.

"Nora, baby, you just don't know..." Detrick found his rhythm and lost himself in her tightness.

5

Sunlight peeked through the blinds and tapped across Lenora's closed eyelids. She lay wrapped within Detrick's body, both of them naked, on the long brown leather sectional. Trying to ignore the sun, Lenora turned on her side and buried herself into Detrick's thick frame. They had lost track of time, between exploring each other, washing one another, and then going at it again until they both passed out.

But Lenora needed to go to work. She sighed as her mind released sleep and her eyes opened.

In front of her, on the coffee table, were stacks of bills that Detrick must have been counting when she interrupted him in the wee hours of the morning.

Detrick's eyes were already open; he was looking at the ceiling as if he were going over a mental checklist of things to do.

"I got to go," Lenora said.

"You can stay a minute." Detrick smacked her bottom. "Always trying to rush off somewhere."

"Unlike somebody up in here, I actually work a job."

"Go on with that." Detrick lit the cigar in the ashtray next to the couch and took a puff. Lenora sat up and inhaled the smoke. "I work, too."

Lenora leaned back and looked at her leg wrapped around Detrick's. It was a good thing she had thought to shave; she hadn't planned on coming over here and getting it in like that.

It reminded her of the real reason for her visit. "There was something that I had to tell you, which was why I came over here like that."

"You mean without calling first?"

"Yeah, you are stuck on that, I see. What you got going on that's got you so funny-actin'?"

Detrick exhaled. "Whatever."

"You better check your other bitches, Detrick, if it's like that. If I'm knocking on the front door, they need to be creeping out the back window."

"Ahh, you like that, huh?

"Don't act like you don't know." Lenora smiled at the silly expression on his face.

"It ain't like that, Nora." He said her name slow and playful. "I always want to know when to expect someone, don't just be having anybody drop by my crib. You know it."

"Yeah." Lenora took a puff of the cigar as Detrick held it between his fingers for her. "The job you gave us last night was a fucking mess, Detrick. Tandy is charging double."

"Double what?"

"Double the fee. Forty, she said."

"Forty g's?" Detrick laughed. "I'll be damned. Glad I ain't stuck with that."

"What?"

They stared at each other for a moment, confusion wafting in the air between the two like thick smoke.

"What are you talking about?" Lenora said.

"What are you talking about, ma?" Detrick sat up and handed her the cigar.

"Detrick, the job you had us do—it was all fucked up."

"That's where you got me fucked up, Nora—I ain't give y'all no job."

Lenora sat straight up. "What?"

"Naw." Detrick lay back down. "Check with Tandra."

"Listen, she said to tell *you* double. After she called you an asshole, again. So I know she was talking about you. What the fuck?"

"I be's that," Detrick said, imitating the hook to the Redman anthem. "Tandra got it fucked up, though. Asshole or not, I ain't give her no job yesterday." Detrick shrugged again. "You hungry?"

Lenora shook her head no. "You better not be fucking with me, Detrick, just trying not to pay. I ain't going back to Tandy looking stupid."

"Never that, baby girl. I wouldn't do you like that."

They lay in silence for a long time. Lenora tried to figure out what was going on. Tandra had said charge Detrick double, but Detrick clearly had no idea what she was talking about.

"You want some breakfast?" he said, after a long while.

"No." Lenora rubbed his stomach. "I can't eat after that mess I cleaned last night. It was too much."

"Damn, that bad?"

Lenora nodded.

With his eyes, Detrick followed the trail of smoke that flowed from his lips. "I ain't hear no buzz about nothing going down last night."

"That's wild." Lenora closed her eyes, trying to forget the faces of the bodies from the night before. She had tried to keep from looking at dead folks when they cleaned—tried to just do her job and keep herself unattached—but she was never able to. "She said it was Crown's spot. You should have at least heard something about it."

Detrick sat up. "What?"

Lenora hesitated. She didn't talk about her cleaning duties with anyone. But Detrick was her man, kind of sort of. He could be trusted. And she needed to confide in someone about it or she was going to explode.

"I know for a fact it was Crown's spot, cuz Tandra said it. And she said to charge you double for it."

"Crown called in a cleanup without telling me?" He sat back, the cigar burned in his mouth without him taking a puff. "Who all was up in there?"

"I didn't know them." Lenora shrugged. "Lots of bodies, though, more than most."

"Yeah," he said it easily, as if the knowledge were no big deal to him.

Lenora looked at him, trying to figure out what he was thinking. But his gangsta mask was in place now; there was no reading the facial expression or those deep black eyes. His nonchalance eased her tongue—he didn't seem worried about it, so she kept talking. Lenora figured that since it was Crown's place, Detrick would know about it sooner or later, anyway.

"Yeah, couple of 'em was killed execution-style. One's neck was slit. It was all fucked up. Those motherfuckers raped this girl, though, so I ain't have no pity on none of them."

"What?" Detrick stared at her. "You found a dead girl up in there?"

"I guess you could say that." Lenora wiped at her eyes. "She was pretty. Light-brown, brown eyes. Long weave, professionally done. At least six hundred for the hair and all. They had her handcuffed to the bed."

"Damn." Detrick looked straight ahead. "What the fuck—"

"Tandra didn't think she had been raped. I don't know what was with Tandy; you could tell the chick had been fucked up, Detrick.

Blood was everywhere on her. She looked so fucked up, I couldn't believe it." Lenora's eyes watered. "I have seen some shit in my life, but I ain't never seen nothing like that. Tandy wanted to dismiss it, just cuz the girl had track marks on her arms. But even a fiend is somebody's momma or daughter or something. I tried to ask the chick what had happened—"

"Wait, she was alive?" For the first time, his mask was gone, replaced with a look of panic. "I thought you said she was dead."

"Huh?" Lenora felt her heart dropped. She had said too much. Way too much.

Detrick pressed, his hands clenched Lenora's thigh. "What she look like, again?"

"Normal. I mean pretty."

"Long hair. Tracks on her arms. A tattoo on her wrist?"

Lenora blinked.

"Did she have a tattoo of a bracelet that said—?"

Lenora could see the tattoo in her mind's eyes, the beautiful delicate ribbons intertwined with the scripted colored words: "Poetic Justice Reigns Eternal?"

"Fuck!" Detrick's roar sent a chill of panic through Lenora. He was up, off the couch, grabbing his cell phone.

While he punched numbers in the phone, Lenora ran over to her clothes. She had been sloppy to wear the same clothes over there that she had worn to the scene of the crime. Breeze would kick her ass for that alone. And the thought of putting the clothes back on made her blood curdle. But she couldn't stay, that much was clear. Detrick was acting like a madman, dialing and texting.

Detrick dug another phone out of his pants pocket and dialed. "Jose, get at me, man. Call me back as soon as you get this message." Detrick left another voicemail.

Lenora strapped her heat back on her thighs.

"Detrick, what's happening?"

"Nora, some shit went down between me and Crown. Me and my men…we are on our, on my own. I don't know. I got to make sure that wasn't my peoples up there." He left another voice message for another person. "Not my girl." Detrick's deep voice was soft and light, like he was talking without oxygen.

"What?' Lenora's mind felt scrambled. "Your girl?"

"For real…" His tone rose as if he were completely out of patience with her. "This ain't even time for that type of shit, Nora."

"No, I mean, you think Crown would do this to you—to your crew?"

Detrick didn't answer. He gave her a look that told her she was still the naïve little girl that he always teased her about being.

Detrick scrambled to the coffee table and pulled out the narrow drawer. He pulled out the guns that lay in the drawer and sat them on the table amongst the stacks of paper. Then he snatched out another phone and dialed as he jumped into the jeans that lay on the chair. "I got to go. I got to check on her and she ain't answering her phone."

Lenora's hands trembled. She remembered Breeze standing there weighing out her options at the job, recalled the turmoil in Tandra's eyes. Truth be told, Lenora didn't want any static from either Breeze or Tandra; both of them were professional to a fault and she would have to kill them or be killed if word got to them that she had run her mouth. "Detrick, listen, I wasn't supposed to tell you nothing about that spot. You can't say nothing to no one about what I just told you. If it ever got back that I said something—that I told…"

"Lenora, that shit ain't nothing to me right now—"

"No, listen. You can't ask Crown about the shit; you can't say nothing to no one!"

Detrick ignored her as he pulled on a jacket over his T-shirt.

Lenora rubbed her eyes. "What if it was...your girl? What are you going to do?"

Detrick met her question with eyes of black steel. Terror flooded Lenora's veins like a needle full of heroin.

The phone rang. "Youngun, where the fuck you at?" Detrick screamed into the phone, spit flying from his mouth. "Where the fuck are Jose and Will? Wasn't they supposed to hook up with PJ last night at the spot? I told them I ain't want her to go alone. What the hell happened?"

Lenora tucked her cape under her arm and headed for the door.

"Hold up, Nora." He stretched out a hand at her as he spoke back into the phone. "Go over there and see where the fuck they at. I'm about to go to PJ's mom's spot. Yeah. Get back at me."

Lenora hesitated and then kept walking.

"Was the girl alive or dead, Nora? When you got there...was she alive?"

Lenora didn't respond.

Detrick ran after her. "When you got there, was she dead or alive?"

"What does it matter, Detrick? We cleaned the scene. Like we always do."

"Shit, shit, shit, shit." He pounded his fist against his forehead.

Fear spread through Lenora's chest like a shot of nitrogen. He was losing his mind; this was a side of Detrick she had never seen—had never wanted to see.

"You know Jose, you seen him over here. Was he in there? What about Will?"

Lenora just stared straight across the room.

"Tell me something, Nora. Say something."

"I don't know." Lenora shook her head as tears ran down her face. "I honestly didn't look at all their faces. I just know the girl. I remember the girl."

"Hold up..." Detrick ran into the kitchen. Lenora inched closer to the door. She heard drawers open and close and then he was back, moving faster than she had ever seen. He held out a photo.

Aw shit. Lenora's heart stopped.

"Is this her?"

Lenora knew without looking that it was the girl. Of course it was her. How else would life play this out; there was no way it wouldn't be her. Lenora's tongue had just started a damn war, one that would have been fought anyway, but that she wouldn't have been a part of if she had kept her mouth shut. Now she had placed herself, Tandra and Breeze right in the middle of some shit. Unless she could talk Detrick out of revealing his source.

One look in his deranged face verified that trying to get him to contain himself would be a waste of time.

"I don't know," Lenora mumbled, pushing the photograph away and opening the door. "I got to go."

"Fuck that." Detrick slammed the door shut and grabbed Lenora by the back of her neck like a puppy.

"Ow!"

Detrick dragged her back into the house. "You ain't going no fucking where."

"Detrick, you're hurting me!"

Detrick's eyes clicked; he seemed beyond understanding anything Lenora said. The ruthless man in him, the one that Lenora had only heard rumors about, had entered the room; the playful Detrick she had spent the last few hours sexing had vanished.

Detrick put his face so close to Lenora that her eyes crossed. He pressed his forehead against hers until the pressure became painful. "You fucking telling me y'all killed her? What about my other peoples. You just cleaned them away like they was fucking trash?"

"Detrick, I swear, I don't know who they was and they probably wasn't even your folks. Wait and see if your people call back."

"You hear any of my phones ringing back? Huh? My peoples gets back at me. Immediately. They don't make me wait. You know that."

Lenora stood in pain, tears running down her face. She moved her head back from Detrick, despite the tight grip. Her fingers clawed at his large hand. He blinked and looked at her as if he realized who she was for the first time. She thought about the Glocks strapped to her legs, but that wasn't even an option. Detrick was her man. Well, kind of. And she would never pull a weapon on him or do anything to hurt him. He was just acting out right now, just caught off-guard. But the feelings she felt for him ran deep. Flashbacks of his whispered promises snapped through her mind when he was taking her from behind last night, when he touched places in her essence that even the Lord Almighty had never entered.

Detrick was, in some ways, her god.

He dragged her back into the house. His movements were jerky; Lenora tugged, trying to get away, and bumped her chin in the doorway. A few steps later, her hip painfully knocked against the coffee table.

"Detrick, please, please let me go."

Detrick yanked her around to face him and changed his grip to the front of her neck and looked at her like a crazy man. Lenora didn't recognize him. She might have to hurt him, but she didn't want to. She didn't know if she had it in her to do it.

His cell phone rang. He released his grip and pointed at the chair across from the couch without saying a word.

Lenora rolled her eyes, her mouth turned down in a frown. *Fuck him for acting like this.* She plopped down in the chair and stared at her hands. They were shaking. She could see Breeze's gray eyes in her mind; she could remember the cold determination in them.

"PJ was talking to Crown last night? Where? What the fuck... what was he even doing there—he don't go to Mira's spot? Who she left with? Oh no..."

Lenora was in a world of trouble; she had a better chance of running out of quicksand than escaping Detrick's house. And she didn't want him mad at her; she wanted him to understand that she had no choice, that it wasn't her fault. She wanted to be his girl, to have him this concerned about her, to love her this much.

Her own weakness turned her stomach. Lenora swallowed the bile collecting at the back of her throat. She was pathetic. Some small part in the back of her mind knew that she was simply turned out; that Detrick was nothing but another man and she needed to use the guns resting on her thighs to end the chaos before it even got started. If she simply pulled the trigger now, no one would ever know. Breeze would never know she had talked, Tandra would never know how weak she really was. No one would know she had violated the rules by sleeping with a client. Detrick's counterattack on her, Breeze and Tandra, Crown, or whoever the hell he was planning to hit, would be stopped.

It could all end now with a single bullet to his dome.

Lenora watched Detrick talking on the phone, stared at the perfect curve of his wide shoulders stretched under the T-shirt, observed his narrow hips and the jeans that fell just right across his butt. He was a thing of physical perfection. His tongue licking her inner thigh flashed in her mind, the look of ecstasy across his face when he released filled her head. Some part of him loved her; he just didn't realize it.

She couldn't kill him. She wouldn't. Detrick's world was falling apart and he needed her right now.

6

"I don't want no damn tortilla chips, Lele." Breeze leaned back on the large red velvet lounge chair. "How many times we got to come to this restaurant."

Lele breathed deeply. "Breeze, this is my favorite spot. You know it. Why are you acting so ill?"

Breeze ignored her and glanced around the restaurant. She dropped a couple hundred in here a week, because it was where Lele insisted on eating for lunch. During their couple time. When Lele demanded Breeze cut off the entire world for at least an hour and relax with her.

Breeze glanced at her diamond-encrusted watch. Lele's hour was almost over.

"You could act like you want to be here." Lele's voice was quiet and soft, not the normal powerful energy Breeze was used to.

"It's not like that." Breeze felt ashamed. Just a little bit. Lele held her down in ways nobody else ever had; she loved Breeze unconditionally. And Breeze was a damn mess; she couldn't help herself. When someone attracted her, she had to sample it. When she wanted something, she had to have it. If she needed to go there, she had to be there. Her needs and demands were endless, because she refused to deny herself anything. A childhood of struggling, her late teen years of hustling and having to out-gangsta the men in her crew, had taken their toll. Since she worked hard, she damn sure played hard. Any other person would have left her alone. But not Lele, sitting here with her funky haircut with blond highlights, lip gloss sparkling and a body-fitting dress with a jean jacket and high-heeled boots. Lele held on and kept herself looking good for Breeze and demanded Breeze squeeze herself into this relationship mode, which fit Breeze like a shoe two sizes too small.

But for her effort alone, Breeze would do it for her. She would do anything for Lele.

"I'm tired, ma. That's why I'm grouchy."

"I know." Lele drank the rest of her margarita. "I have my own needs, too, Breeze. And it's not fair to you for me to keep binding you down."

"Binding me down?" Breeze scooted closer to Lele and laid her head in her lap. The cool thing about the restaurant was that each table was its own intimate lounge area with a coffee table in front. She had full access to Lele's hourglass figure. "What do you mean?"

"I mean this. How I am dragging you to my favorite spot and you don't want to be here." Lele stroked Breeze's hand with her palm as she looked into her eyes. "Don't try to front. You hate it here."

"No, I don't." Breeze closed her eyes and felt the rhythm of Lele's blood pulsing through her veins. "I'm here, ain't I?"

"But that's the thing, Breeze. I don't want to be in a relationship with someone who is just here."

Breeze's eyes opened. She and Lele had done this dance before. Lele wasn't going anywhere. "Why are you starting this now?" Breeze's phone beeped. She looked at the screen and saw the code 312. It was Tandra.

"You going to take that?"

"You want the bill for this food paid?" Breeze didn't look up at Lele as she sat up and called Tandra.

No answer from Lele as she dug into her purse. Breeze ignored her, keeping her eyes on the female bartender wearing the thin pink T-shirt while the phone rang.

Lele pulled out her lip gloss and freshened it, then she checked out her hair in her small compact.

"Hello." Tandra's voice sounded heavy. She was wearing herself thin.

"What's up?"

"I can't find Nora."

Breeze glanced over at Lele who was now also looking at the bartender and glancing back and forth between her and Breeze. The vibe was thick, Lele must have sensed it. Breeze pointedly kept her eyes on the bartender, anyway—Lele would have to accept it.

"Why are you looking for her?"

She heard Tandra sigh and also heard her heels clicking against the pavement. "I got to meet with Crown. I wanted Lenora there with me. Two is better than one."

"Especially when y'all go in looking like a couple of femme fatale divas. That's always good for business."

"Either way," Tandra said, ignoring Breeze, "I can't find Nora. After last night, I don't want her out of pocket too long."

Lele pulled out a hundred-dollar bill and sat it in the billfold. Breeze eyed it and glanced at Lele, questioning. She had to have some twenties in her purse instead of the hundred-dollar bill. Lele ignored her, standing up and adjusting her dress.

"What you have in mind, Tandy?" Breeze needed Tandra to get to the fucking point. Lele was up to something, Breeze could feel it. This wasn't the time to play babysitter, either; Lenora had better get it together.

"I don't want to go to Crown's spot with nobody backing me, Breeze."

"You want me in on the meet?" That was a first. Tandra had never asked before. Breeze didn't know it had bothered her until just now, when the question had finally been asked. She should have been asked before now. But, then again, Breeze had a clear defined role in this thing. The business belonged to Tandra and the way Tandra ran it had kept their pockets full and their jobs coming in steadily.

"No." Tandra didn't even pause. "Breeze, what the fuck do you think? Yes, I want you there. But not in the meet with Crown. I need you to make sure I get in and out. I was going to ask you to come with us, anyway; I feel like you need to be there. But it's just gonna be me and you."

Breeze was silent. The brief sting of disappointment at not being in the meet was drowned out by Lele, swaying her hips as she seductively moved to the bar and took a seat.

"Ain't this some shit?" Breeze said under her breath.

"What, Breeze? I can't hear you."

"Nothing. I didn't say nothing."

"Okay, can you meet me in thirty minutes? At the warehouse. Drive something else, not your joint and not the van. I want you to keep an eye on things while I am in there."

"No problem. Thirty minutes." Breeze slapped the phone closed, her eyes locked on Lele talking to the bartender. Lele slid the bartender a piece of paper and then she held the bartender's hand and wrote on her wrist. The bartender's curly hair seemed to bounce along with the vibrant music; her eyes never left Lele's hips. She reminded Breeze of a black Betty Boop.

Breeze stood up. Lele pulled away from the bartender and walked to the door. She put her sunglasses on before she stepped through the heavy glass doors. She never looked back at Breeze.

"This bitch." Breeze looked around for the waiter. She had to go, but she wasn't leaving the waiter with that hundred-dollar bill. She needed change and then would give a tip.

As her eyes scanned the large room, she noticed Betty Boop walking toward her with a huge grin on her face. "You must be Breeze."

"Depends." Breeze wasn't interested in playing games at the moment; the bartender was no longer important. She had to get outside to Lele and cuss her out for how she was acting.

"On what?" The bartender smiled again. She wasn't taking the hint.

Breeze tucked her hands in her pockets and locked her steel-gray eyes on the bartender. "On who's asking and why."

"Well, I am Jessica. And Lele asked me to bring this to you." Jessica smirked as she handed her the note. Breeze took it, ignoring Jessica's smile as she walked away.

You take what you want. I am doing the same.

Breeze balled up the note in her fist. She snatched the hundred-dollar bill from the folder and dropped two twenties and a ten on the table instead. She didn't have time for Lele and her games right now. Breeze walked out.

7

During the day, a nightclub is the emptiest space in the world. People fill the space, working and preparing for the night to come, but it seems like the skeleton of what the club really is, the opposite of when it is pulsating with moving bodies and hypnotic rhythms.

Club Enjami was no different. It was one of Crown's spots, the space where he happened to be most of the time. Tandra knew she could find him there. She wanted full payment for her trouble the night before and she wanted her money immediately. She didn't have a relationship with Crown and wasn't going to risk falling victim to "out of sight, out of mind" bullshit as it pertained to her money.

Walking up to the three-story warehouse, she glanced over her shoulder at Breeze sitting in a dark black Cadillac. The real owner of the car would be pissed when he discovered his ride was gone. Tandra couldn't see Breeze, but it was good knowing that she was there, that Tandra wasn't alone.

"Can you hear me?" Tandra whispered without moving her mouth as she stepped into the cool space, hoping the small microphone hidden in her collar was working

"No doubt." Breeze's voice sounded small and computerized. It didn't matter; at least they could hear each other.

Tandra adjusted her short red wig, checked her lipstick in her reflection in the glass, and pulled open the door.

As soon as Tandra stepped into the warehouse, she felt blinded.

It took a quick second for her eyes to adjust to the dark atmosphere. A lady in all black came over to her. "May I help you?"

"Yes." Tandra looked around the room, but didn't see anyone of obvious power in her space. "I need to see Crown. I have an appointment," she lied.

The girl looked her up and down and then, accepting her story, said, "Follow me."

Tandra walked behind the small girl and took in the feel of the club. A couple of people were laughing and talking to each other. A girl with twists in her hair was dancing alone to the quiet music playing in the background. Two men moved lounge furniture around to better accommodate the expected crowd.

The girl stopped in front of a short man whose long locs were pulled back into a neat ponytail. He wore the vest and pants of a three-piece suit; his expensive pink shirt was flattered by a pink, blue, and gold tie. He looked at her questioningly as the waitress nodded and walked off.

Tandra was surprised; she had been expecting bodyguards and an entourage of men, which was why she wanted to bring Lenora. The two of them together, dressed to kill and exuding sensuality, would give off an image of mystery. By herself, Tandra hoped she could still maintain that professionalism and get the benefit from it that she needed.

"May I help you?"

"I am not sure," Tandra said, as she again glanced around the club. "I am here to meet Crown."

"And you are?"

"Tandra. We have business to discuss."

The man nodded; his face blank. Tandra continued, without showing any emotion. "I own a cleaning business."

"Tandra." His English accent kicked in and he stood straight up, returning to a stature of royalty. She realized that he had purposely changed his accent and stance as a cover. "I know you."

"So you *are* Crown."

"How is it we haven't met before?" He moved closer to her, taking her hand in his and leading her to a table in the rear of the club, away from the few people working and the couple of people just lounging.

"No reason to. I don't like to pay clients a visit; I prefer to have payment worked out before my duties are carried out."

"Of course you do." He observed her like she was entertainment. "So, how do you want to do this?"

Tandra's hand floated near her Beretta. "What do you mean?"

"I mean, what are you charging me and how do you want your money?"

Really? Tandra glanced around the club again. Rarely was anything this easy in life. What was the catch? "I am charging you forty for the mess you left."

Crown winced as he pulled out her chair. Tandra didn't want to sit down, but had no way out of complying with him. She slid into the seat and he sat across from her.

"Did I hear you correctly?"

"Yes, you did. The fee is double, plus expenses. Your people left an unnecessary mess. We had to remove furniture, paint and the count was..." Tandra raised her hands to show eight fingers.

"But that is what you do."

"No." Tandra crossed her legs. Crown watched her legs with appreciation; his slight smile turned Tandra on. She tried to ignore it. "What I do is make sure that the scene is evidence-free. That's easy enough with a low count and unnecessary brutality." Tandra leaned forward. "When someone participates in a bloodbath, there are additional expenses."

Crown sat back and observed her. "I like you."

"That is irrelevant."

"No, it is very relevant. It makes all the difference in the world."

Tandra stared at him as he smiled at her.

"How do I know it's been handled?"

"Send someone up there to check it out if you want. I don't care. I won't be going back."

Crown nodded his head. "Do you have anything for me?"

"All residue has been eliminated."

"I am willing to pay thirty. For your trouble."

"Sixty and the price will go up with every counteroffer." Tandra stood up. "Don't waste my time and please don't disrespect my professionalism. I take what I do very seriously; it is not a discount service to be negotiated down."

"And if I don't pay?"

Tandra shrugged and kept her game face in play. If he didn't pay, then a few of the bullet casings that she had would find their way to the police and that was for damn sure. That evidence wouldn't be buried in final until she was paid in full. But she wouldn't tell him that. He would find out the hard way what the consequences were, and it would be in a way that he couldn't prove her responsible and couldn't directly retaliate against her.

"Oh, so you keep insurance for yourself, huh?"

Tandra met Crown's eyes. "Sixty-five then?"

"Please, sit down, sweet lady." Crown laughed and clapped his hands. A thick woman with evil eyes approached and grimaced at Tandra, who didn't acknowledge her with anything more than a glance.

Crown mumbled something to her and she walked away. "So, Tandra, what do you drink?"

"I don't." Tandra was ready to go.

"What are you doing this evening?"

At the direct question, Tandra smiled and met his eyes. "I am sure I will be working."

"Cleaning?"

Tandra shook her head no. "Cleaning is not my only business."

"Ah, an entrepreneur." The woman returned and dropped four stacks on the table. "I like a woman with some grind."

Tandra rolled her eyes.

Crown smiled. "Forty grand, then?"

Tandra weighed her options. She met his smile with a sweet one of her own, but her eyes were deadly serious. "Forty is no longer on the table—it was my initial offer and you forced me to have to counteroffer."

"Let's meet in the middle, Tandra. You can do that, right?"

Tandra considered it. She nodded.

Crown raised one finger. The woman with the evil eyes appeared and dropped another stack on the table. She rolled her eyes at Tandra as she walked away. Tandra laughed out loud as Crown shook his head.

"My assistant is territorial."

"I see." Tandra shook her head. "It's no problem." Tandra stood again, preparing to leave.

"So, Tandra, why don't you enjoy Club Enjami sometime? VIP. On me, of course."

Tandra smiled. She needed a night out. Maybe she would bring Lyell and Lenora and tell Breeze to bring Lele. They could pop bottles and just relax. "Maybe. When would be a good night?"

Crown stood up and placed his hand on her waist. "Tonight, of course..."

"I'm not sure about tonight. I would want to bring some friends."

"Maybe this weekend, then?"

Tandra gave Crown a flirtatious grin. He was sexy. Tandra pointed to the stack of money on the table. "Can you give me something to put that in?

"Of course, Sexy." Crown raised a hand again.

The evil-eyed woman appeared again with a purple leather handbag. At the same time, Tandra saw someone walking toward her, his motion smooth but purposeful; too focused for someone in a club in the middle of the day. He bumped into a waiter and walked across the center of the dance floor. His eyes were on her and Crown.

Tandra's instinct sounded off like a three-bell alarm. She didn't know why, but her hands reached for her Beretta. Crown's eyes widened, his jaw fell open.

The man raised the gun. The first explosion stunned the people in the room; everyone stood still for a second until the evil-eyed woman screamed as blood squirted from her shoulder. Bodies were in motion after that. Crown grabbed for Tandra, but she would be damned if he used her as a human shield. She lunged past him as a second shot rang out and hit the floor behind the table. Her gun slid from her fingertips under the bench behind her.

"Crown, you son of a bitch!" The gunman screamed; a blood-curdling sound that made Tandra's heart drop to her toes.

She knew that voice.

8

The several people that had been milling about before broke for the door at the sound of the first shot. Tandra and Crown were trapped, too deep in the club to get past the gunman. The gunman smiled at Crown; he had the advantage.

Bodyguards that Tandra hadn't noticed before emerged from the shadows of the club. The dark man fired and hit the tall man running toward Crown from the bar; another bullet nailed the shorter guard who had been talking with the waitress by the kitchen. The second shot hadn't come from the gunman; a female dressed in all black had shot him.

A female who came running out of the kitchen with a gun; the gunwoman in all black shot her. The woman in all black ran into the kitchen and Tandra could hear her blasting her gun to clear the room. The shot woman fell close to Tandra, who tried to crawl closer to get her gun.

"Bitch, don't move." Tandra felt the heat from the gun near the back of her neck. She lay still facing the floor and spread out her arms. The gunman took the gun from the victim, whom he shot in the face.

Tandra didn't blink.

"Crown, you're finished. You hear me."

"Detrick, this is a foolish move." Crown's smooth voice contained no fear, in fact he sounded like he was laughing. Tandra couldn't believe it was Detrick who was shooting up the place. She turned her head to better focus on the man in the dim light. It *was* Detrick. *Shit*. Whatever this was, it had nothing to do with her. She figured it was time to make her exit.

Tandra stood up.

Detrick glanced at her, his face questioning her boldness, until he recognized her. "Tandra. The red hair threw me off. I didn't know that was you."

"Detrick, I don't have anything to do with what's going on here." Tandra took a step toward the door.

"Oh, you don't?" Detrick kept his gun trained on Crown, but Tandra had his full attention. "Actually, I am glad you're here. I can get some fucking answers now."

"What?" Tandra shook her head; he had her twisted. There was no question that she had the answer to where it concerned him.

Crown interrupted, "Detrick, what the hell are you thinking, huh, to pull some shit like this on me? On the Crown?" His accent made his words faster and choppier. "I made you. And you cross the Crown?"

Detrick shot Crown in the thigh. Crown whimpered as the force of the shot knocked him to the ground. "You tried to kill me and my crew."

Crown didn't answer, his teeth clenched as he grabbed his leg.

"You thought I wasn't going to know. You hired them damn Cleaners to cover your trail. So, what, you were going to take us all out? Just like that, Crown?"

Tandra's eyes flitted between Detrick and Crown. How did Detrick know about the job? How had he found out who was in the apartment?

The female in all black stepped out of the kitchen, her gun drawn. Tandra knew, without looking at her, that it was Lenora. The puzzle pieces fell into place. Her heart stopped beating for a second and sadness flooded her. Lenora had talked and had walked in like Detrick's do-or-die bitch.

Tandra met Lenora's eyes. Lenora's mouth opened, shame clouded her face. "Tandy, I didn't know..."

"Lenora, what did you do?"

Sweat poured down Crown's brow. "This is one of your people?" Crown gasped.

Tandra nodded.

"You fucked up," Crown whispered. "You fucked up, sexy lady."

Tandra met his eyes.

Detrick pushed past Tandra to stand directly in front of Crown. "It didn't have to be like this. I told you I was doing my own thing. You should have let me go."

"You stole from me. You don't steal and walk away." Crown dragged himself to a chair and sat down.

"I didn't steal from you, Crown. I learned the game and used it, the way you did. That ain't stealing."

"You cut a side deal. And didn't offer up any tax on it to me or to those who have embraced you." Crown spat phlegm at the floor. "You are a thief, dumb bombaclot." The words curled around Crown's tongue like a marble in his mouth. "And now, now you are a dead man."

Detrick shrugged. "I was a dead man, anyway, right? It was just a matter of time. But you crossed the line. PJ? *My* son's mother? You did that?"

Crown shrugged. "She was nothing but a low-paid trick. And the pussy was a tad bit raggedy, anyway." He laughed; a weak sound of fury. "I figured I would fuck her one last time before I let my boys get a taste. Let her do what she specialized in before she took her last breath." Crown sized Detrick up, his eyes traveling up and down his body. "And look at you. Supposed to be a man, standing here signing your own death sentence over a fiend." Crown pressed his fist against his thigh. "Pathetic."

Detrick stared at him as if he didn't hear a word Crown had said. Instead his lips moved, like he was having a private conversation with himself. He nodded his head, lifted the gun and riddled Crown's body full of bullets. Tandra flinched, but didn't move. She was going to distract Detrick out of his trance, that was for sure.

She met Lenora's eyes again; this time her own eyes were blank. Emotion had been wiped clean. Lenora was now an enemy and would be handled like one.

"What did you do, Nora?"

"I didn't know you were going to be here."

"You sure about that? I called you a hundred times. Or did you decide you were going to come in during the meeting and do me, like he just did Crown."

Detrick snorted at Tandra's comment. He stood over Crown and stared at him. "Your empire is mine now. Trust."

"Tandy, listen to me, I went to Detrick's like you said. To ask for double for the cleaning. But he ain't have nothing to do with the cleaning. He just put it together."

No explanation would matter to Tandra. Maybe Lenora didn't realize that. "You went over there in the same clothes, Nora. Then you come up in here wearing them? With all the bodies you touched and all the shit we cleaned, you still wearing the same fucking clothes?" Tandra's normal calm broke; she could hear herself screaming.

"I was just trying to let him know that you wanted double."

"You fucked him?"

Silence. Lenora looked at the floor.

"I am going to ask you again. Did you fuck my client?"

"It's wasn't like that."

"Enough of the bullshit, Nora. Just tell her." Detrick pushed his gun back in the side strap and pulled out a cigarette.

"Tell me what?" Tandra crossed her arms and stared at Detrick, who smiled at her.

"I been fucking Nora for months," Detrick said with a shrug. "She a'ight."

Tandra laughed, her eyes glinting fury. "See, Nora, I told you he was an asshole."

"No doubt." Detrick lit a cigar and took out his cell phone and called someone. "Come to Enjami. Now," he demanded.

When he hung up the phone, he and Tandra looked at each other and shook their heads in unison.

Lenora looked back and forth between the two as if she were left out of some sick joke. Why was she never included in the silent conversations that happened all around her? It was obvious they thought she was a fool, some little errand girl who didn't deserve any respect.

"I'm a'ight?" Lenora faced Detrick. "What the hell does that mean?"

"Shorty, I'm not feelin' it right now. You need to take it down."

"What it means, little girl, is that he is simply fucking you. And in the process of getting fucked, you put my business at risk."

"That's all you care about, Tandy? Is your business?"

Tandra ignored her and looked at Detrick. "Why are you coming in here blasting like this?"

Detrick bit his lip. "I've known you forever, Tandra. That's why I can't even be mad. Not really. Was PJ up in that spot?"

Tandra shook her head. "I don't know who PJ is."

"A girl was up in there alive. The little girl told it." Detrick didn't bother to look at Lenora, either. "She was mine, Tandra."

Tandra bit her lip. "I didn't know. It would have been different, Detrick, had I known." She moved closer to him. "You know that, right?"

"Who did it? Who pulled the trigger?"

"I did." Tandra didn't hesitate. She looked him in his eye, power for power, respect for respect. "I'm not going to lie to you. I did it."

A moment of silence passed between them. Tandra wasn't going to apologize, because she wasn't at fault. It was part of the job, part of the life. And Detrick understood that.

"This one here." He pointed at Lenora without looking at her. "Loose lips, Tandra. You got to be careful with her."

"Fuck both of y'all." Lenora had her guns drawn, pointing at Detrick and Tandra.

Tandra felt her body temperature rise; her anger was making her blood boil. Detrick chuckled.

"Put that gun down, Nora," Tandra said.

"No, I am sick of both of y'all. I am not stupid. I'm standing right here and y'all gonna act like I ain't even in the room—"

Detrick moved quickly, his gun trained on Lenora. "If you point a gun at me, you better be prepared to use it, stupid bitch!"

Tandra shook her head. "Don't do this, Lenora."

Detrick chuckled, dropping his gun to his side. "Fuck this little girl." Detrick turned his back on her and walked toward the bar. "I need a drink."

"You gonna turn your back on me?" Lenora's hand began to shake as a tear tumbled down her back. She hiccupped and shrieked at the same time. Tandra knew the look of craziness that crossed her face; the look of pure desperation just as a woman's heart breaks.

"Lenora, no!"

Tandra lunged at Lenora and bumped her arm just as she fired at Detrick's back. Another shot rang out into the air. Lenora gasped in surprise as the bullet hit her in the back and shoved her body forward with its momentum. She stumbled and looked down at her chest; blood trickled down the front of her body suit, the hole squarely between her breasts.

"Oh shit." Detrick fell forward; the bullet had penetrated the back of his arm. "Did this trick just shoot me?"

Tandra looked around, trying to figure out where the shot that hit Lenora had come from.

Tears covered Lenora's face. "Tandy?"

Another shot hit Lenora in the back of the head. Tandy stepped toward her as Lenora fell into her arms.

Breeze stepped out of the shadows, smoke trailing from the tip of her gun.

Tandra stared down into Lenora's blank eyes.

Detrick rubbed his hand over his face.

The three of them said nothing for a long while. Detrick stood up when his cell phone beeped and started walking across the dance floor to the door.

"Tandra," Detrick said just before he walked out, his voice quiet. "I need this scene cleaned."

Kai is the author of the highly acclaimed urban fiction novel, Daughter of the Game. *She is also receiving critical acclaim for the novel* The Loudest Silence, *a chilling and raw examination of the death of love.*

A published and nationally recognized poet and writer, her poem, "Pre-Destiny," was featured in the April 2008 issue of Essence *magazine and she was a*

Featured Poet in A Place Of Our Own (APOOO) national tribute in April 2008 and RAWSISTAZ Author Showcase, April 2007. Kai is a contributing poet in Step Up to the Mic: A Poetry Explosion, *by Poetic Press (Xpress Yourself Publishing). A winner of the No Candles Infinity Contest, hosted by Osbey Books, Kai is credited for writing emotionally raw and thought-provoking works and has been published in numerous anthologies and magazines under other pen names. Her highly anticipated sequel,* Daughter of the Game II: The Secret Keeper, *is now available. An alumni of Hampton University, SUNY Brockport and Georgetown University Law Center, she is a licensed attorney and proud parent. For more information, visit the author at www.authorkai.com*

THREE THE *Hard* WAY

BY C.J. HUDSON

1

Roni and Kita sat in a stolen Chevy Trailblazer and watched the front door of their mark intently. At any minute, it would swing open and all hell would break loose.

Roni and Kita were members of the Get Money Bitches, three cold and heartless women who were about making paper by any means necessary. Whether it was carjacking, spot-rushing, or strong-arm robbery, the Get Money Bitches were all about clocking the dough. During their last spot-rushing heist, an unexpected problem had arisen and their leader, Jasmine, had to pump three hollow points into the owner of the house.

The fact that he wasn't supposed to be there in the first place contributed to his own demise. During the GMBs' week-long casing of the house, they had learned that the man and his wife consistently left the house together every Friday night around seven and didn't return until after nine. But on this particular day, the GMBs arrived to their surveillance spot just in time to see the couple's car pulling out of the driveway. They assumed that the couple was together, but they really couldn't tell since the BMW 325 had tinted windows. So when the GMBs made their move and broke into the house, they were surprised to see [illegible]
his recliner. He was startled awake when Kita acc[illegible]
over a lamp.

The man, too brave for his own good, made a lunge toward Jasmine and got rewarded with three slugs to the stomach from a weapon he never actually laid eyes on. His wife had forgotten her purse and pulled back into the driveway in time to see the GMBs flee through the backyard. She couldn't see Roni's and Kita's faces but clearly made out Jasmine's. Her husband died two days later and now Jasmine was on trial for first-degree murder. Her attorney recommended copping a plea to a lesser charge, but the GMBs had other ideas.

Blunt smoke filled the cavity of the truck as Roni and Kita passed the get-high-stick back and forth. Roni looked at a picture of the mark again and shook her head.

"Damn," she said. "I can't believe that we about to dirt a piece of ass this fine. I shuda asked Jasmine if I could rape this bitch first."

"Roni, don't start that gay-ass shit," Kita said. "You lucky I'm even lettin' yo pussy-eatin' ass hit this blunt."

Roni laughed as she checked the clip in her AR-15 assault rifle. She had been bisexual since her fifteenth birthday, when her drunken gay aunt snuck into her room that night and gave her a birthday present she would never forget. Roni was five feet seven inches tall and built like a brick shit house. She kept her hair in Chinese bangs and wore gray contact lenses. With the exception of a cut on her left shoulder, her cinnamon-colored complexion was scar-free.

"Bitch, please," Roni said, snatching the blunt out of Kita's hand. After taking one last hit, Roni focused her eyes on the door and waited for it to open.

"You need dick in yo life, bitch," Kita teased, "to open up that tight-ass coochie."

Roni gave Kita the finger. Whereas Roni was bisexual, Kita was all woman and was always down for the dick. On more than one occasion, she used her angelic face and perky breasts to woo a mark. With long, flowing, golden hair and butter-light skin, most men were pure putty in her hands when she decided to turn on the charm. Kita's head snapped around when she noticed a slight grin fall across Roni's face. Their mark had emerged from the building wearing a blue scarf wrapped around her head and large Gucci sunglasses covering her eyes.

Roni slowly lowered the passenger-side window and pointed the weapon at the woman. Her finger twitched as she observed the woman walking toward her BMW. The woman looked annoyed and they understood why. Earlier that morning, after the woman had left to meet with the prosecutor, Kita had fixed her garage door so it wouldn't open, making it necessary for her to park on the street. Deciding to change the plan at the last minute, Roni took the gun off of the woman and pointed it at her tires.

"The fuck you waitin' on, bitch?" Kita asked. "Dirt that hoe!"

Roni ignored her friend and waited for the woman to get inside her car. As soon as she did, Roni let off two quick shots that flattened the front and the back tires. Before the confused woman could even realize what was going on, Roni jumped out of the car and sprinted toward the car. The terrified woman stared down the barrel of Roni's assault rifle. She never had a chance to scream for her life as Roni pumped round after round into the driver's seat.

Glass shattered and decorated the street as pedestrians ducked for cover, diving behind trees and cars in an attempt to get away from the insanity unfolding on the city street. After dumping about thirty rounds into the state's star witness, Roni ran and jumped back in the stolen vehicle. She was barely inside before Kita peeled off, burning rubber down the street.

"Bitch, what the fuck is wrong with you?" Kita screamed. "You tryin' ta get us knocked or somethin'?"

After placing her weapon on the back seat, Roni calmly lit up a Newport, took a drag, and blew the smoke into the air. "Kita, them scary-ass muthafuckas ain't gon' tell on nobody. Let's dump this fuckin' truck and keep it movin'."

Kita shook her head. Her friend was starting to get reckless. She made a mental note to talk to Jasmine later on. They needed to get a handle on that before it ended up costing them all their freedom.

2

Jasmine Turner picked her fingernails as she sat next to her lawyer in Cleveland's Municipal Court. She smiled slightly as she cut her eyes to her right and noticed the beads of sweat that had formed on her lawyer's forehead. Motioning for her lawyer to lean over to her, Jasmine softly whispered in her ear.

"Take it easy, Melissa; everything's gon' be straight."

Melissa Crawford looked at her client like she was crazy, but the more she thought about it, the more she realized that her client had indeed been accused of some crazy things over the past year. "Jasmine, they have a fuckin' surprise witness to this charge. How the hell can you be so calm?"

Jasmine simply winked her eye, then turned around and smirked at all the nosey people who had come out to witness her receive her just due. No one would look her directly in the face except for one light-skinned redhead with large sunglasses, who was staring intently.

The fuck this bitch staring at, she thought.

Not giving it a second thought, Jasmine turned back around and continued to look good. Jasmine appeared nothing like the cold-blooded killer that Cleveland made her out to be. With an olive complexion free of blemishes combined with a model's figure, she looked like she should be on a runway instead of in a courtroom. Her light-brown, marble-like eyes were captivating and her smile could melt the North Pole. Her shiny, black hair was tied in a ponytail that hung right above her shoulders. Jasmine and her lawyer jumped as the prosecuting attorney suddenly slammed a stack of papers down on the table. He had received a note from a uniformed officer standing guard in the hallway.

"Your Honor, may we approach?" he asked.

Judge Green beckoned the two attorneys toward the bench. Melissa looked back at Jasmine, who in turn, shrugged her shoulders in an innocent "I don't know" gesture. No sooner had the judge and the two officers of the court disappeared into the back when a sly smile escaped Jasmine's face. She knew exactly what the note said and the severity of the message conveyed.

$ $ $

"What?" screamed the prosecutor. "What the hell do you mean, the witness was killed?"

Judge Green looked at the prosecutor through beady little slits. "First of all, Mr. Morgan, I'd watch my tone if I were you. Either you think that I'm your wife or you have definitely taken leave of your senses, but either way..." The judge pointed his index finger squarely in the face of Jason Morgan. "Watch how you talk to me!"

The apologetic look on Mr. Morgan's face said it all. The last thing that he wanted to do was piss Judge Green off.

"I'm sorry, Your Honor. It's just that without that witness—"

"Without that witness, you have no case against my client." Melissa was elated to finish his sentence for him.

The hateful glare the prosecutor gave Melissa had her practically giddy on the inside. Now she understood why Jasmine was so confident about the outcome of her trial; the witness would never make it to the courtroom.

"I hate to sound crass, Mr. Morgan, but it was your witness' refusal to accept a police escort that led to this incident." Judge Green seemed extremely upset about the entire thing. "If she would've pushed her pride aside and let the system work for her, we wouldn't have this little dilemma."

"Your Honor, I don't think we have any choice but to move for a dismissal," Melissa said. "As the prosecutor so elegantly put it, without the witness, their charges cannot be proven."

The judge was stuck; Melissa was right, but he didn't like it. In his heart, he wished that there was something that he could do, but his hands were tied. There was no way that the state would win this case without their star witness. The case was built on circumstantial evidence as it was, so without Juanita Chandler to point the finger at the women she saw running from her house, the case essentially collapsed. Judge Green was no fool. Years of experience on the bench told him that Jasmine's crew had something to do with Juanita's sudden demise. Since there was no way to prove it at the moment, he had no choice but to grant Melissa's wish.

"Look, I'm sorry, Mr. Morgan, but Mrs. Crawford is right. Without the witness, I have no choice but to dismiss the case."

The prosecutor stormed out of the chambers in a huff. Normally, when someone showed him up like that, Judge Green would hold that person in contempt, but he felt the frustration on this one.

"And you, Mrs. Crawford," he said, pointing his finger at Melissa. "If I find out that your client had anything to do with that poor woman's death, I'll make sure that her and anyone else involved gets a lethal injection! Do I make myself clear?"

"Yes sir, your honor," Melissa said, walking out.

Judge Green, feeling like shit even though it wasn't his fault, shook his head and followed her out.

$ $ $

Judge Green plopped down in his seat after he reentered the courtroom. Taking off his glasses, he ran his right hand across his face in a manner that said he was fed up with the shenanigans of the legal system. Before he spoke, his eyes scanned the courtroom, knowing full well the chaos that was about to ensue after the announcement he was about to make. As soon as his pupils got to Jasmine, his head stopped rotating. His cold stare would have intimidated the hardest of criminals, but Jasmine Turner was a different breed. She was a thoroughbred and not easily scared by such tactics. A sly smile escaped her lips as Judge Green shook his head at her with disdain.

"Ladies and gentlemen of the jury," he began. "I have received news of a terrible tragedy. It appears that there was a fatal shooting involving the witness. I have no choice at this time but to dismiss the case. Ms. Turner, you are free to go. Court adjourned," he said, banging his gavel.

The courtroom erupted. Jasmine covered her mouth and feigned shock and remorse.

"Oh my God," she said loud enough for the judge to hear her.

Judge Green knew it was an act, but there wasn't anything that he could do about it. "Order!" he demanded. "Order! Order in my courtroom!"

Jasmine kept her hand up to her mouth, more so to conceal a smile than anything else. She turned around and looked at the shocked crowd mumbling amongst themselves. Her eyes came to a rest on the same redhead that she'd caught staring at her earlier. Once again she ignored her and turned back around.

"Congratulations," said her lawyer. "You beat the rap."

3

The humidity index made the eighty-degree heat feel like ninety-five and the GMBs were just as hot as they stepped out on the town to celebrate Jasmine's release. Ever since the judge had denied bail, Jasmine had been cooped up behind bars for the better part of two months. She couldn't wait to get out and let her hair down. Kicking it with her crew was one of the things that Jasmine had missed most. The last time she'd kicked it with her partners-in-crime, she and Kita had to pull Roni off a bitch's ass for disrespecting them.

Roni beat the girl so bad that it took a well-placed ten-thousand-dollar bribe to keep her from pressing charges. Jasmine didn't want any of that drama tonight. All she wanted to do was kick back, drink, smoke a couple of blunts, and chill with her homegirls. The GMBs walked past the crowd and up to the door as if they owned the joint.

Jasmine allowed her friend to get by. "Okay, Kita, do ya thing, homegirl."

Kita wasted no time. "Hey, Terry, baby. How you been doin'?"

"I'm straight," replied the stone-faced bouncer as he tried to throw shade.

"Baby, you ain't still mad about last month, are you? I meant to call you, but my baby daddy been havin' a bitch on lockdown and shit. Hell, I ain't even been able to wipe my ass without that nigga being there."

"Is that right?" the burly bouncer asked. "I see yo ass all up in this bitch tonight though," he added with much skepticism.

"That's because that nigga back locked up again. I'll tell you what, boo. I owe you, but I swear on everything if you let me and my friends in—"

He didn't wait for her to finish. "Sorry, y'all gotta go to the back of the line."

"You sure about that, boo," Kita said, letting her hand graze his dick.

The way he tensed up told her that all she had to do was take it home. She got on her tiptoes and whispered in his ear. Before she was even done telling him about all the nasty things that she would do to him, he was removing the velvet rope and allowing her entourage to enter. Haters looked on in jealousy and disgust but held their tongues. A few of the people standing in the line had already heard about the GMBs and didn't desire any trouble. Jasmine and Roni mean-mugged the haters as they walked past the smiling doorman.

"Damn, bitch, how many blowjobs did you promise that nigga to get him to smile like that?" Roni asked.

"I merely told him that I was gon' give him a little somethin' later on."

"Nasty bitch," Jasmine remarked.

"Don't hate, homegirl, don't hate."

The GMBs made their way through the club amidst the usual eye rolls by women and lustful stares by men. Jasmine and Kita garnered most of the looks as Roni was on the prowl for some fresh pussy. Club Ice was a rather small club but VIPs, big ballers, and shot-callers regularly fell through, in large part because of the star power and reputation for serving strong drinks and being a trouble-free spot.

"What can I get for you ladies?" the long-faced bartender inquired.

"Aye, yo, let us get a bottle of Cristal, dawg! We celebrating tonight." Jasmine beamed.

"Oh yeah? What we celebrating?" he asked in a friendly tone.

Before Jasmine or Kita could say a word, Roni spoke up. "We," she said, pointing at him and her girls, "ain't celebrating shit. Me and my homegirls are celebrating. Stop being so fuckin' nosey and get the damn bottle."

Jasmine and Kita looked at each other and then at Roni.

"Roni, what the fuck is wrong with you?" Jasmine asked. "Homeboy was only makin' conversation."

"Conversation, my ass. That hoe-ass nigga was all up in our business."

"Roni, you need to chill the fuck out," Kita said. "Ain't nobody tryin' ta get into no silly shit with yo ass tonight."

"Damn, bitch! You act like you scared or something. You *skurred*, bitch?"

"Look, you clit-lickin' dyke! Ain't no fuckin' body scared! Yo ass be on some dumb shit sometimes!"

"Bitch, who the fuck you think you talkin' to like that? You must think I'm one o' them lame-ass niggas you be fuckin' wit!"

"Ahight, that's e-fuckin-nough!" Jasmine was tired of the verbal sparring between her partners. "Roni, Kita's right. We don't need to be getting into no bullshit tonight. We came in this bitch to have a good time, so let's have a good time."

"Yeah, ahight." Roni sucked her teeth. Feeling double-teamed, Roni got up and stomped toward the bathroom like an upset child.

"Jas, you need to talk to that bitch. I'd hate to have to slap the shit outta her ass in here."

Jasmine burst out laughing. "Bitch, please. It ain't enough muthafuckas in here to get Roni off yo ass!"

"Whatever!" Kita dipped her hand into her purse. When she pulled it back out, she was clutching a pearl-handled switchblade. "I'll carve her ass up in here!"

Jasmine stopped laughing immediately. She didn't care about them arguing, but she drew the line at them doing bodily harm to one another. "We don't hurt each other; we hurt the enemy," Jasmine sternly said.

"Damn, Jas, I was playing."

"Uh-huh."

"Anyway, you really need to talk to her. She altered the plan today and could have gotten us knocked."

This got Jasmine's attention. If it was one thing that she hated was doing dumb shit when it came to business. "What happened?"

After the bartender returned and set the bottle of champagne on the counter in front of them, Kita proceeded to tell Jasmine about Roni's stunt. Jasmine felt her temperature rising and when Roni came back, Jasmine's mood had changed.

"Let me get this shit straight, Miss Al Capone. You jumped yo ass out of the cover of a stolen truck in broad daylight and let off rounds? Bitch, are you fuckin' stupid?"

Roni shot an evil glare at Kita, who sat there with a smirk on her face.

"Couldn't wait ta tell it, could you, Henry Hill? Ol' snitchin'-ass heffa. You sure we can trust this hoe, Jas? She might crack under pressure, cut a deal, and dime our asses out!"

Kita quickly gave her the finger.

"Yeah, I do trust her. And I wanna trust you, Roni, but you gettin' a little reckless."

"What you mean, you *wanna* trust me? You don't?" snapped Roni.

"I trust you not to snitch. But like I said, you startin' ta lose focus and we can't be doing no shit like that. Hell, you want all of us to get twenty years?"

Roni sat there, still staring at Kita. She was pissed that Kita had snitched on her.

"Look, Roni, I ain't tryin' ta turn you into a choirgirl. All I'm sayin' is ease up on the crazy shit, ahight?"

"Ahight," she said with a shrug of her shoulders.

"Cool. Now gimme some fuckin' love, homegirls." Jasmine grabbed the two of them in a head lock. "Shit, I just got out; I wanna have some fuckin' fun tonight!"

Jasmine turned up the bottle of champagne and drank it like she hadn't had a drop of liquid in years.

Kita held out her fist to Roni in an attempt to solidify their friendship. "We cool, girl?"

"Yeah, I guess so, bitch," she said, smiling. She was still upset with her but didn't want to ruin the night for Jasmine.

50 Cent's old school jam, "In Da Club," came on and everyone in the place broke their necks trying to get on the dance floor. While Kita and Jasmine played the bar, downing the liquor, Roni went to the dance floor searching for someone to take home. She didn't make it two steps before she spotted a fine, bowlegged, light-skinned thing coochie-popping in the middle of the floor. To her surprise, the girl motioned for her to join her.

She didn't have to ask twice as Roni made her way through the crowd and bounced up on her. The girl quickly put her arms around Roni's waist and pulled her close.

"What's yo' name, boo?" Roni asked her.

"Randi," the woman seductively replied.

"Well, Randi, my name is Roni, and I would just love to take you home tonight and do some things to you."

"Damn, slow down, Roni. We just fuckin' met. I could be a damn serial killer," she said, laughing.

"I ain't worried about no shit like that. I can more than handle myself."

For the remainder of the song the two women rubbed and grinded on each other. Randi's sweet-smelling perfume had Roni hotter than a firecracker. When she reached down, grabbed Roni's hand, and rubbed it across her clit, Roni practically lost it. She wanted to finger-fuck her right there on the dance floor. Randi stopped short of letting Roni stick her finger inside of her. She was teasing the hell out of Roni and Roni couldn't stand it.

I'ma eat the hell outta this pussy tonight, she thought.

When the song was over, Roni invited her back to the bar so she could meet Kita and Jasmine. They had already killed one bottle of Cristal and were now working on a second one.

"Damn, y'all finished with that entire bottle already?"

"Girl, you know we don't fuck around," Kita said.

Jasmine eyed Randi suspiciously. She didn't like meeting new people because she didn't trust many people. When Roni took a little too long to introduce her, Jasmine cleared her throat.

"Oh shit, my bad, Jas. This is Randi. Randi, these my homegirls, Jasmine and Kita."

"Sup?" Kita said dryly.

Jasmine looked at Randi and cocked her head to the side. "Don't I know you from somewhere?"

"I doubt it," Randi said. "I'm new in town and this is the first time I done had a chance to get out."

Jasmine stared at her for a minute. She couldn't put her finger on it, but she was sure that she had seen this bitch somewhere before. When nothing registered to her, she simply shrugged her shoulders and held out her hand. "Nice to meet you."

Kita grabbed the bottle and poured Randi a glass of champagne. "Well, since you here, you might as well have a fuckin' drink with us."

"Thank you."

As the four women talked and drank, Roni couldn't seem to take her eyes off of Randi. Every now and then Randi would rub up against Roni, teasing her on purpose. She was leaving no doubt as to what her sexual preference was. Tired of the games, Roni made her move.

"Yo, ma, you ready to bounce? Let's blow this joint and go have some real fun."

"What?" Kita jumped in. "Damn, Roni, our homegirl just got outta jail and you tryin' to roll out on us early for a lick of the clit?"

"Kita, you really need to mind yo muthafuckin' bidness!"

Randi snickered under her breath. She thought it was funny how the two friends were arguing amongst each other.

"I gotta take a piss," Roni said, before storming off to the bathroom.

As soon as she left, Kita turned a cold stare on Randi. "You mind tellin' me jus' what the fuck is so funny?"

"I wasn't laughing." Randi attempted to suppress a smile.

"Bullshit! You think I didn't hear that little snicker? You may have my girl twisted, but I don't trust bitches I don't know."

Crossing her arms and leaning back in a defiant pose, Randi stared Kita dead in the eyes. "And I don't trust hoes that talk shit to me and don't know me."

Before the situation could escalate any further, Jasmine stepped in and calmed her friend down. "Kita, cool out."

Reluctantly, Kita backed down. She didn't know or trust this broad, but she also didn't want to make the crew hot by fucking up some bitch in a club.

Jasmine turned her attention back to Randi. "I apologize for my girl's outburst, but we grew up together and she just don't wanna see our friend get hurt."

"I understand." Randi matched Jasmine's stare. "I'm not trying to hurt anybody. I'm jus' lookin' for a good time." Randi reached into her back pocket and pulled out a piece of paper with her cell phone number on it. "And I certainly don't want to come between lifelong *friends*."

The way she said *friends* instantly told Jasmine that she was trying to be a smart ass, probably assuming that all three women were gay.

"Could you please give Roni this and tell her to give me a call? I really would appreciate it." Randi made sure to hand the slip of paper to Jasmine and not Kita. She knew that Roni would have never gotten it if it were up to her. "It was nice meeting you," she said as Jasmine took the note from her.

Without saying another word, Randi turned on her heel and walked away. When Roni returned, she immediately got mad at Kita, whom she figured had chased Randi off.

"Where Randi go?" she asked, staring at Kita.

"The fuck you askin' me for, bitch?"

"'Cause I know yo ass probably had somethin' to do wit her leaving; that's why!"

"What? Bitch, you crazy! I ain't give a fuck if the bitch left or stayed!"

"You know what?" Jasmine rubbed her temples. "You two bitches are really starting to get on my nerves. Let's jus' call this shit a night, get together in the morning, and map out the next hit. Matter of fact," she said, thinking, "since we didn't get a chance to finish that last job, let's hit that bitch up in a couple o' nights. We can't do it right now 'cause the PoPo gonna be all over that bitch for the moment. But it should be cleared out for the taking in a few days. We can hit the bitch late night. It ain't like it's gonna be somebody there. We can roll in around two-thirty in the morning, get our snatch on, and roll the fuck out!"

"Why so late at night, though?" Roni asked.

"Because by that time, the nosey-ass neighbors should be asleep and we don't have to worry about them calling the man and tellin' 'em that somebody is rambling around in the house where two murders have taken place!"

"That's what's up," Kita said. "The Get Money Bitches are back in effect!"

"Here. Sandy, or Randi, or whatever the bitch name is, left you her cell number." Jasmine handed Roni the slip of paper.

After sliding the note into her pocket, Roni, along with the rest of the crew, decided to raise a toast to getting more money. Roni's mind, however, was moving in a slightly different direction. With the sweet scent of Randi's perfume still lingering in her nostrils, she almost came on herself thinking about tasting her.

4

Randi watched through hateful eyes as the GMBs left the club. She smirked as she watched the tipsy women half-walk, half-stumble to their rides. It would be easy to take out one of them tonight, but she was determined to stick to her plan. She wanted the entire crew to suffer.

As Roni pulled into the flow of traffic, Randi followed three car-lengths behind her. When Roni finally pulled into the driveway of her rancher-style home, Randi made a mental note of the address and kept going. Roni would have no idea that she was being followed. Jasmine was a clever bitch and would have picked up on being tailed in a heartbeat. Kita was so paranoid that she would have been looking in the mirror the whole time so Randi made the wise decision to follow the weakest link. She would soon use her pussy to make Roni even weaker.

As soon as Jasmine entered her living room, she realized something wasn't right. Everything seemed in order, but Jasmine wasn't buying it. Her senses were still sharpened and being in jail had done nothing but honed them even more. She calmly reached into her purse and palmed the nickel-plated three-eighty she kept in there. Then she slowly and quietly removed the pumps that she had worn for the evening. Holding the pistol down by her side, her heart began to race as she heard movement in her bedroom and noticed that the lamp on her nightstand was on.

Easing up to the door to her bedroom, Jasmine pushed the door opened, aimed, and fired. The naked man that was lying in her bed grabbed the pillow from the other side of the bed and covered his head as if that would keep the bullet from shattering his skull.

"Gotdammit, Jasmine!" screamed the man as Jasmine cracked up laughing. "You tryin' ta give a nigga a heart attack?"

"You trying ta make a bitch shoot yo dick off?" Jasmine countered. "I keep tellin' yo ass to let me know when you gon' be all up in my spot. I also remember tellin' yo ass earlier that I was gon' be kickin' it wit my girls and that I would text yo ass when I got home, Tony."

"Woman, yo ass coulda killed a nigga!"

"How many times do I have to tell yo ass that I never keep one in the chamber? That's how muthafuckas accidently shoot they fuckin' self. Now, like I was sayin', nigga. Didn't I tell yo ass to let a bitch know when you was gon' be chillin' in my spot?"

"Yeah, I know, baby. I just couldn't wait to get some of that sweet-tastin' punany. Shit, it's been over two months. Plus, I didn't want my wife to hear my cell phone buzz and start trippin'."

Jasmine popped her lips as she put away her gun. "Nigga, please. You ain't been worrying 'bout what that bitch say. Why you worrying 'bout it now?"

"Jasmine, she's my wife. I can show her some respect."

Three seconds of silence was followed an outburst of laughter by both parties.

"Yeah, okay," Jasmine said. "And when is the last time the bitch let you fuck her?"

Before Tony could answer, Jasmine strutted into the bathroom and closed the door. She didn't mind sharing Tony for the time being; she was too busy with trying to make a come-up to be bothered with a clingy-ass man. As long as he provided her with some quick, eleven-inch dick and useful information, she was more than satisfied. Just thinking about Tony lying in her bed with a rock-hard dick got Jasmine's juices to flowing. It had been over two months since she felt the penetrating stabs of Tony's thick anaconda between her thighs. After taking a quick shower, Jasmine rubbed Tony's favorite vanilla-scented fragrance all over her body.

She eased into the bedroom wearing nothing but a smile, which soon turned into a frown when she realized that Tony had fallen fast asleep. Walking over to the bed, she looked down at him and had she not been so horny, she might have let him sleep so she could get her laugh on. Tony had no idea he was doing so but, every now and then, he would talk in his sleep. Jasmine eased into the bed next to him and slipped her hand under the covers. Her head soon followed the same path as she gently kissed and licked the mushroom-shaped beginning. Tony's dick instantly hardened in her hand. When she glanced up from beneath the sheets, Tony was smiling down at her.

"You slick muthafucka. Yo ass wasn't 'sleep."

Tony simply shrugged his shoulders and continued smiling. Getting back to the business at hand, Jasmine slowly wrapped her MAC gloss-coated lips around Tony's dick. The gentle suck on the head caused involuntary muscle movement in his toes.

"Oh shit!" She let the shaft travel halfway down her throat. By the time she got it all in her mouth, Tony's nutsac was ready to explode.

Sensing the eruption coming, Jasmine stopped abruptly.

"Hey! What the fuck you doing, baby?"

Tony's question was quickly answered as Jasmine mounted him. For the next fifteen minutes, Jasmine rode Tony's dick like a cowgirl.

"Oh shit, baby! Oh God, baby, here it comes!"

Jasmine wasn't far behind. "Ah shit!" She screamed as two months of backed-up cum poured out of her and painted the sheets as well as Tony's dick.

The warm feeling of Jasmine's love fluids caused Tony's love javelin to become hard once again.

"OOH SHIT!" she screamed.

Without pulling out, Tony somehow flipped Jasmine over until they came to rest in the missionary position. Jasmine wrapped her legs around Tony's back and hooked them at the ankles while Tony drove every inch into her dripping sex hole.

"Oh shit! Oh, hell yeah, baby! That's it, baby; beat the shit outta this pussy! Fuck, baby, I'm 'bout to cum again!" she yelled as she dug her fingernails into Tony's back.

Tony tried his best to hold out, but Jasmine's pussy was too good. Five seconds after Jasmine came for the second time, Tony followed suit and squirted thousands of sperm cells inside Jasmine. Jasmine wanted to kick herself in the ass for not making him use a condom, but it was too late to bitch about it now. For the prior three months before she got locked up, he had been begging her to let him hit it raw. Now he had finally gotten his wish.

The two had almost drifted off to sleep when his cell phone rang and abruptly jolted them wide awake.

"I bet I know who that is," Jasmine teased.

After checking the caller ID, Tony took a deep breath. "Hello," he cautiously answered.

"Nigga, what the fuck you mean, hello? You know what fuckin' time it is? Where the fuck are you?" his wife yelled through the phone.

"Does it matter where I am?" he responded. "You kicked me out of the house, remember?"

"I didn't kick you out of the fuckin' house. I told you that if you weren't going to treat me right, then maybe you should find yourself some other place to lay your fuckin' head. That's not the same as kickin' you out and you know it, asshole!"

"Look, I'm tired of fighting with you. That's why I checked into a hotel tonight. I didn't feel like the fuckin' headache."

"Oh, so I'm a fuckin' headache to you now, huh?"

"Woman, that's not what the fuck I said."

"Then what are you saying, Tony? Why do you keep treating me this way? What the fuck have I done to make you disrespect me this way? You know what? Fine! If you wanna stay in a hotel tonight and fuck whatever whore you're lying up with, fine. But remember, Tony, I'm your wife! The little bitch that you're laying up with isn't!"

"Why do you always assume that I'm with another woman?"

"Because I know your ass, Tony!"

"Whatever. I'll see yo ass in the morning."

Before his wife could say another word, he hung up on her. He turned on his side and noticed that Jasmine was staring at him.

"What?"

"Nothing," she said as she let her hand travel down to his balls. Cupping one of them in her hand, she squeezed gently. The smile then left her face as she increased the pressure.

"Hey! What the fuck you doing?" He started to squirm.

"I heard that whore comment your wife made and I suggest that you check the little bitch. Unless you want me to do it."

"No, I'll take care of it," he said.

"Good. 'Cause I would hate to have to put a hot one in Melissa's ass."

5

Roni slammed her fist down on the table as she continued smoking her morning blunt. She had called Randi three times since last night and had gotten the voicemail each time.

"What the fuck kinda game this bitch call herself playin'?"

Roni wanted a piece of Randi in the worst way. She could still smell Randi's perfume when she had awakened that morning. Not being able to taste her sweetness was driving Roni crazy. Taking a puff from her blunt, Roni sat back and imagined all the nasty things that she was going to do to Randi. Having nothing on but a wife beater and a pair of boxer shorts, Roni slid her hand inside the shorts and began to finger herself.

She slowly rubbed her clit as she thought of the way Randi looked out on that dance floor, grinding against her. As she was about to reach her climax, her cell phone rang. *Whoever it is just gonna have to wait*, she thought.

After releasing her love juice, Roni looked at the missed call on her cell phone. "Fuck!" she said when she realized that she had missed Randi's call. She immediately called Randi back, but once again it went to Randi's voicemail.

"Fuck! How I keep missin' this bitch?" She set her phone back on the table and took another puff off the get-high stick. Roni was becoming increasingly frustrated. All she wanted to do was lick some clit, suck on some tits, and cum a little bit. When her cell rang a second time, she snatched it off the table and answered it without checking the ID.

"Randi?"

"Bitch, do I sound like that hoe?" screamed Kita. "Don't you got caller ID on that raggedy-ass phone?"

"Fuck you, Kita. What the hell do you want?"

"Roni, we had a meeting today, remember? You were supposed to meet us at Landmark thirty minutes ago, homegirl."

"Landmark?"

"Yeah, Roni. The restaurant on Fifty-third and St. Clair. Damn, girl, where the fuck yo head at?"

"Oh shit, I forgot," Roni said, as if a light suddenly clicked on. "Tell Jasmine I'm on my fuckin' way."

After quickly washing up in her sink, Roni threw on a pair of sweatpants, a T-shirt, and an old pair of Reeboks and dashed out the door. After closing the door behind her, she looked back and noticed that there was a slip of paper taped to it. She snatched the paper off the wall, read it, and shook her head.

Damn, baby, you hard to get a hold of. Why don't you meet me at the Club Odyssey on St. Clair at 2:30 so we can get better acquainted? That way it will be just me and you and ya girls can't run interference. Randi.

Roni smiled on the way to her whip, thinking that she was finally gonna get to taste that pussy.

$ $ $

"Roni! Get your head outta that bitch's ass and listen to what the fuck I'm sayin'," screamed Jasmine. "We gotta be on point with this shit. Them muthafuckin' dope boys ain't nothin' to be playin' around with. If we gonna do this shit, we have to have our shit together."

For the last ten minutes, Jasmine was trying to map out in detail how they were gonna rob a couple of the hood's package slingers. The ones that they were planning to rob weren't super big-time yet, but they weren't small potatoes either. One of them happened to be the doorman from the club that they were in last night. Kita had screwed him and had come up on some eye-popping information by eavesdropping on his conversation.

Roni's mind had been wandering ever since she got to the meeting. As hard as she tried, she couldn't seem to keep her mind off of Randi. It had never been this hard for her to pull a bitch before, but Randi was making it a challenge for her.

"Oh my bad, Jas. I jus' had a rough night and didn't get too much sleep; that's all," she lied.

Kita popped her lips and rolled her eyes to let Roni know that she didn't believe a word.

"Like I was sayin'," Jasmine continued. "Kita, I want you to get both of them muthafuckas to meet you at your apartment about forty-five minutes before they're supposed to make the buy. Make sure that either the front or the back door is left open."

"How the hell is she gonna pull that off?" Roni asked.

"Don't worry 'bout that, homegirl; I got this," Kita said with a smirk on her face.

"Roni, make sure you bring the guns with the silencers on 'em."

"What time is this shit jumpin' off?" Roni asked.

"At three-thirty. Why?" Jasmine asked suspiciously.

"I was jus' wonderin'. Shit, I gotta know what time to meet you at the house, don't I?"

"We ain't meetin' at the house this time. I got something I gotta take care of in a minute, so I'll jus' meet at the corner of Kita's street."

Immediately, Roni started thinking about Randi and whether she could somehow get in touch with her and get in a quickie.

"What? You got something else to do?" Kita asked, reading her mind.

"Did I say that I had something else to do?"

Kita threw up her hands. "I was just asking."

"Then stop asking stupid-ass questions."

"Whatever."

Jasmine stared at Roni, then at Kita. "I don't know what the hell is going on with you two, but I'm getting sick and fuckin' tired of y'all actin' like fuckin' children. Get y'all shit together."

Without waiting for either one of them to respond, Jasmine walked out the door. She was so pissed that she didn't even finish the rest of her food. For a few quiet seconds, the two longtime friends sat there and stared at each other. Kita broke the silence first.

"Look, Roni, all I'm saying is that ever since you met this bitch, yo shit ain't been on point. I jus' don't trust the bitch."

"You don't even know her," Roni snapped. As soon as the words left her mouth, she wanted to take them back; she knew exactly what Kita was going to say.

"You don't know that bitch either, Roni. Shit, you jus' met her ass last night."

Roni started to speak, but Kita held up her hand before she had a chance to protest.

"All I'm sayin' is be careful. I'm getting a bad vibe from that hoe."

Kita held out her hand for Roni to give her some dap.

Roni pounded her fist and gave Kita a smile.

"I know you got my back, homegirl, and if it makes you feel any better, I'll back off o' this bitch...after I bang her."

Kita shook her head and laughed. "Girl, yo' ass is something else. Let's jus' make this paper."

$ $ $

Randi sat on the corner of Fifty-third and St. Clair in her Jeep Liberty smoking a Kool and staring out the window. It would be so easy to exact her revenge right then and there, but she was determined to see the plan through. She watched as Jasmine walked out of the restaurant with a pissed-off look on her face. Then she watched ten minutes later as Roni and Kita came out and went their separate ways. Looking down at her watch, she saw that it was almost eleven o'clock.

The cell phone on her hip vibrated and when she unclipped it, she saw Roni's number pop up on the screen. Laughing at the way she had made Roni suffer from not answering her calls, she decided to answer this one.

"Hello."

"Damn, about time you answered the phone. I been tryin' ta call yo' ass all morning."

"I'm sorry, baby," Randi said. "Didn't you get the note that I left for you on your front door?"

"Yeah, I got it and...hold up a minute. How the fuck did you know where I lived?" Roni asked suspiciously.

Shit, thought Randi. She could kick the shit out of herself for that dumb move. Thinking fast, Randi mixed truth with lies. "To tell you the truth, baby, I followed you home last night after the club. I wanted to surprise you and stop by your place for a nightcap, but I got scared. I shouldn't have followed you like that, baby. Please don't be mad at me. I promise, I'll make it up to you," Randi said, hoping that Roni would fall for her little performance.

"Yeah, okay." Roni tried to sound unenthused. The truth of the matter was that she was so excited she was about to cream on herself. "But we need to meet an hour earlier than we had planned. Some shit came up that I have to take care of."

Randi smiled a wicked smile as an idea quickly formed in her head. "Okay, that's cool, but listen. Can we meet at your place instead of the bar? I have somethin' that I really need to show you, baby," she said seductively.

"What you got to show me, girl?"

"It's a sweet, sweet surprise, baby. I guarantee you will like it."

Just hearing Randi talk like that had Roni moist already. "Ahight, but at two-thirty, I have to roll."

"Don't worry. It won't take that long. See you at one-thirty, sweet thang."

Roni hung up and smiled from ear to ear.

6

Kita opened the door wearing nothing but a sheer red robe and a smile. "Bring yo' sexy ass in here, baby." Terry eyed her like a piece of candy. "Where ya boy at?"

"Oh, he's coming. He had to grab something from the trunk. We got about an hour and a half to kill and then we got a power move to make."

"You know, baby, it's only because I love you and want to prove it to you that I'm even doing this shit, right? My dude would fuck me up if he knew what I was about to do for yo' big-dick ass," she said, stroking his ego.

"Fuck that nigga. If he was on point wit' his hustle game, then his silly ass wouldn't a got knocked. Where yo' kid at?"

"Oh, my mom has him," she lied. Kita didn't have any kids.

A few seconds later, Terry's boy, Ray, came walking through the door with a look of sheer lust on his face. He was carrying a large duffle bag and the bulge in his jeans told Kita that she was going to have a hell of a time trying to stall them.

"Man, where you want me to put this? Damn, nigga, she fine as fuck!"

"You like what you see, Ray?" Kita did a one-eighty and gave him a view of her ass.

"Hell yeah." Ray rubbed his crotch.

Terry and Ray had unknowingly and unwittingly fallen into Kita's trap. Terry was so mesmerized by Kita's beauty and body that it had never occurred to him to ask her how she knew Ray's name. After taking him back to her place and screwing him silly, she played sleep while he went in the other room to talk on his cell phone about a cocaine buy. He foolishly talked about when, where, how much, and what time. She had already heard through the grapevine that Terry and Ray liked to run trains on girls around the way so she decided to use his lustfulness against him.

Seeing her opportunity, Kita wooed Terry into thinking that she had fallen in love with him and wanted to do this to prove her love. In reality she was merely setting him up to be robbed. She stole a quick glance at the clock and saw that it was two-thirty. That meant that she had an hour of stalling to do before her girls came and stopped the show.

She went into the kitchen and poured three drinks. She had thought about drugging them, but then remembered that Jasmine said that it would be harder and more noticeable if they had to drag the bodies out. When she came back into the living room, the two of them had removed their shirts and were smoking on a blunt.

Kita grinned. "Yo, let me hit that shit."

After puffing and passing three times, the men were ready to fuck. Terry grabbed Kita and pulled her down onto his lap. His hard-on immediately made Kita moist. She didn't mind giving Terry some pussy. It was Ray's nasty ass that she didn't want touching her. She glanced at the clock again and did a double-take when she saw how much time had passed.

After making up an excuse to go into the kitchen to unlock the back door, she mumbled to herself, "Where the fuck these bitches at?"

$ $ $

"Yo, Roni, check it out. There's been a change in plans. Instead of meeting me at the corner of Kita's street, go to this address."

Roni reached over on the nightstand and jotted down the information Jasmine was giving her.

"Okay, here's what's up," Jasmine said. "I followed Terry's baby mama and his daughter to they house. Go over there and do a snatch and hold until you hear from either me or Kita. If the mother tries to get gung ho up in that bitch, then do the damn thing. But hold off on the girl, feel me?'

"Yeah, I got chu."

Roni was trying her best to keep her voice even while she was talking to Jasmine, but Randi's tongue traveling along her thighs was making it difficult. Roni moaned softly as Randi's wet mouthpiece slithered underneath her right knee, across her dripping wet cunt, and across her left leg.

"You like that shit, baby?" Randi asked.

"Oh, hell yeah, baby. Please don't stop."

Randi grabbed Roni's inner thighs and gently pushed them apart. Stealing a quick look at her alarm clock sitting on her nightstand, Roni knew that she had to hurry up and cum so she could go and take care of GMB business. Her thoughts of getting money were temporarily put on hold as Randi dropped her head in between Roni's legs and pushed her tongue inside her vagina.

"Oh shit," cooed Roni.

Randi's tongue worked magic as it danced around Roni's pulsating clit. When Randi gently bit down on Roni's clit causing a pleasure/pain sensation, Roni screamed in delight. "Oh shit, you good pussy-suckin' bitch, you!"

Randi began to flick her tongue faster and faster across Roni's clit and just when Roni was about to climax, Randi abruptly stopped.

"NO! NO! NO! Baby, what the fuck you doing? Oh God, baby, please don't stop," Roni begged.

Before Roni could catch her breath, Randi ran into the kitchen, reached inside the freezer, and took out a Popsicle. Then she ran back into the bedroom and ran it across Roni's pussy. Roni's whole body shook as the cool sensation drove her crazy. Randi slid the Popsicle inside of Roni's love box. The sensation of the Popsicle going in and out, combined with Randi's mind-numbing head game, sent Roni over the top.

"Ah shit, baby! I'ma fuckin' cum!"

Once Roni came, she tried to sit up, but Randi had other ideas. Clamping her arms around Roni's legs so she couldn't move, Randi continued to hungrily lap at Roni's treasure chest.

"Shit, bitch, what the fuck you doing to…OH FUCK!" she screamed.

By the time Randi was done, Roni had cum two more times and passed out. When she woke up, Randi was gone, she had five missed calls, and the clock read four-fifteen. Knowing that she had fucked up, Roni yanked the clock off the dresser, threw it against the wall, and picked up her cell phone.

$ $ $

Jasmine angrily picked up the black 9mm pistol that was lying on the passenger seat. After checking the clip and making sure that it was loaded to capacity, she slammed the clip back up inside the base of the gun. For the last fifteen minutes, she'd unsuccessfully tried to reach Roni. She wanted to know if everything was going according to plan. Although she had told Roni to bring the guns, she wasn't about to trust her totally with that. Roni had been acting like a damn schoolgirl with a crush ever since last night. *This bitch needs to get her mind right*, thought Jasmine. *She ain't gonna be fuckin' up my paper.*

Jasmine eased down the street at a snail's pace and stopped when she got two houses down from Kita's place. Looking around for any potential nosey ass witnesses, Jasmine slid out of her whip and walked quickly toward Kita's house.

Not wanting to take any chances, she ducked below the window-sill in case the two marks were sitting in the living room. Jasmine tiptoed up the back steps and cautiously turned the doorknob. The door creaked softly as she continued to push it in. Jasmine shook her head and smiled upon hearing the soft moans coming from Kita's bedroom. *I shoulda known this bitch was gonna get her some dick before we had to murk these muthafuckas.*

Jasmine eased through the kitchen and was about to go past the living room when she saw Ray on the couch smoking a blunt. She stood there for a second trying to figure out what to do. *Fuck! She was supposed to have both of them back there!* While she was debating, Ray stood up and started taking off his clothes. Apparently, Ray wanted to finish smoking his weed before he got busy. With her gun behind her back, Jasmine let out a soft giggle when she saw the size of Ray's love stick. Ray's hearing was better than she thought. In an instant, his head snapped around in her direction.

"Bitch, who the fuck is you?" he screamed.

Before she even had a chance to answer, Ray reached into his pants pocket, pulled out a switchblade, and headed toward her with murder in his eyes. Jasmine's entire plan was falling apart right before her eyes. Now she was forced to react.

"I'ma fuck yo ass—" *Psszpp!*

That's as far as he got as the deafening sound of Jasmine's silencer-laced gun barrel ejected a hollow point and ripped through Ray's chest plate, snapping bone and tearing muscle and cartilage along the way. The impact knocked Ray back into the living room and onto the sandy brown carpet. Blood mushroomed beneath him as Ray stared up at the ceiling. He was dead before he hit the ground. Creeping past the now decomposing corpse, Jasmine made her way back toward the bedroom. The closer she got to the door, the louder the moans became. She peeked inside the room and saw her friend's legs perched on Terry's shoulders. Holding onto his arms for dear life, Kita looked to be in heaven as Terry was blowing her back out.

"Oh shit, baby, that feels good as fuck! Don't stop, baby! I'm about to cum!"

Jasmine hated to do this to her friend, but she had killed a man so they didn't have time for her to get a nut. She walked over to Terry and slapped him upside the head with the butt of her gun.

"Shit!" he screamed as he fell off the bed onto the floor.

"Damn, bitch. You couldn't wait another minute or two for me to get a nut?" Kita asked.

"The fuck goin' on in this muthafucka?" Terry yelled.

Jasmine slapped him with her gun. "Nigga, shut yo' bitch ass up before you end up like yo' punk-ass boy! What the fuck was that nigga doing in the living room, Kita? You was supposed to bring both of dem muthafuckas back here!"

"I know, but that punk-ass nigga wanted to finish smoking his fuckin' blunt."

"Instead of getting some fuckin' pussy? The fuck wrong with that nigga?" Jasmine asked.

"Naw, he figured he would come back and get the pussy after he got good and high. Wait a minute," said Kita as she suddenly realized that it was just the two of them. "Where the hell is Roni?"

"I'on know where that bitch is! I done called her ass four or five times!"

"Man, I can't believe you hoes set a nigga up!"

"Believe it, muthafucka," Kita said, laughing.

"Get yo' punk ass up!" Jasmine yelled.

Kita simply shook her head. She still couldn't believe that Roni was AWOL. "Hol' up. You mean to tell me that Roni's ass is missin' in action?" Kita asked in amazement.

Jasmine glared at her. "Ain't that what the fuck I jus' said? What, you think I'm fuckin' lyin' or somethin'?" Already pissed that the plan was not going smoothly, Jasmine seemed to be taking her anger out on Kita.

"J, I was just askin'. I didn't mean to—"

"You two bitches never mean to," snapped Jasmine. "All y'all been doing is arguing ever since I got the fuck outta— Omph."

Jasmine grunted as she hit the floor. In the midst of her yelling at Kita, she never noticed that Terry had inched his way toward her. When he was sure that Jasmine was distracted enough, he lunged at her and tackled her to the floor. The gun flew out of Jasmine's hand and slid over by the bedroom door.

"You fuckin' bitch! I'ma break yo' muthafuckin' neck!"

Terry grabbed Jasmine around the neck and tried to squeeze the life out of her. He kept an eye to the side in case Kita tried to make a break for Jasmine's gun. Jasmine clawed and scratched at Terry's face but couldn't get him to release her.

Pow!

"Aw shit!" he screamed as heat and pain seared through his back.

Jasmine took both of her hands and with all her strength pushed Terry off of her. Kita fired from her .25 automatic twice more, hitting him in the stomach and groin. Jasmine scrambled over to the door and retrieved her gun. She walked up on the bleeding Terry and ended his pain with a bullet to the forehead.

It took the two of them an hour to wrap the two bodies in plastic, clean up the blood and haul them off to the dumpsite.

While on the way back to Kita's to get cleaned up, Jasmine's cell phone rang.

"Whatever the fuck you about to say, I don't wanna hear it right now!" she yelled into the phone. She knew it was Roni before she even looked at the screen. "Meet us at the bar!" Jasmine hung up without giving Roni a chance to say a word.

7

Roni leaned forward onto the bar with both elbows and rubbed her temples. She had developed a migraine headache as soon as she awoke and realized that she had slept through the job. She quickly tossed back the rum and Coke that she was drinking on and ordered another one. Roni was nervous as hell and the only thing that had ever been able to steady her nerves was liquor. She'd fucked up big-time and she knew it. Jasmine didn't play when it came to her cash so she knew, at the very least, she was going to get reamed out.

"Yo, let me get anotha one."

"Uh, Miss, don't you think you've had enough?" asked the slender bartender.

"Did I ask you fo' yo muthafuckin opinion, nigga? Just fix me anotha fuckin' drink! Shit, everybody wanna play captain save a hoe nowadays!"

"Fuck you then, bitch," he mumbled under his breath.

Just then Jasmine and Kita walked through the door. Jasmine had a murderous look in her eyes. She sat on one side of Roni while Kita sat on the other. After three awkward minutes passed, Jasmine turned, looked Roni dead in the eyes, and said, "Explain."

Roni took a deep breath. She had rehearsed the lie so much in her head that she figured it would be a piece of cake by the time

Jasmine and Kita got there. But now that Jasmine was in front of her, it was a whole different story. Over the years, Roni had seen Jasmine do some unspeakable things. She still cringed when she thought of the time Jasmine slit a four-year-old's throat because her mother was stalling about opening her safe.

"Jasmine, I swear to God, I ain't do this shit on purpose. I was sittin' down in the chair smokin' a blunt and gettin' ready to follow your instructions."

Knowing it was a complete lie, Kita snorted out a laugh. If looks could kill, she would have been on the evening news from the way Roni scowled at her.

"Anyway, I was sittin' there and I fell asleep. I didn't wake up 'til about an hour ago."

"Just enough time to miss all the fun, huh?" Kita teased.

"Shut the fuck up. Nakita!"

The smile instantly left Kita's face. She hated being called by her full name and Roni knew it, which is why she did it in the first place. Jasmine kept staring straight ahead. She called the bartender down there and ordered a drink.

After gulping down half of her Rémy Martin, Jasmine spun around on her stool so that she would be facing Roni directly.

"So let me get this bullshit straight," she said through clenched teeth. "I told yo' ass what to do regarding this job, but instead of being on Ps and Qs, yo' ass is slackin' on ya muthafuckin' pimpin'."

"That's what the shit look like to me."

Before Roni could even start to blow up, Jasmine waved her finger and shook her head, signaling for her to be quiet. "And you," Jasmine said, pointing her finger at Kita. "Shut the fuck up and stop fuckin' instigating."

Kita turned her stool around to face the bar and continued to sip on her drink. Jasmine was so mad that she didn't even remember Kita ordering a drink.

"I called yo' ass several muthafuckin' times! How come you ain't answer the damn phone?"

"I...I didn't hear it, Jasmine. I swear."

In one gulp, Jasmine downed the rest of her liquor and turned back to face Roni. "Well, hear this, carpet muncher! I'm finin' yo' ass a thousand dollars for almost fuckin' up the job! Get yo muthafuckin' shit together!"

Jasmine hopped up, slammed the glass down on the table and walked toward the door. Luckily for Roni, it was a very slow day and there were no customers in the bar as of yet, or she would have been one embarrassed woman.

"I'm going home. You two bitches meet me at my house tomorrow at seven o'clock sharp," she said, staring at Roni as she spoke. "Roni, take Kita home tonight! I wanna be alone."

Roni's and Kita's eyes connected and before Kita could say something fly, Roni was all over it. "Don't say shit! If yo' ass say one damn word, you walkin' the fuck home."

Kita ordered another drink and smiled. She didn't have to say a word.

$ $ $

Randi sat back with her feet kicked up on her coffee table. Picking up the pack of cigarettes that lay in front of her, she shook one out, put it up to her lips, and fired it up. She smiled as she blew the toxic smoke into the air. Their plan was working to perfection. All she had to do now was take it home.

Her cell phone buzzed, interrupting her thoughts. She let it buzz a couple more times before she decided to answer it. After pressing the talk button and saying hello, she listened for a few seconds and then said, "Yeah, I got it all under control. I'm going to put that plan in motion tomorrow. By the time Jasmine figures out what's going on, it'll be too little, too muthafuckin' late."

Randi paused for a minute before asking, "So, what yo' sexy ass got on?"

Click.

Randi laughed as the caller hung up on her. Feeling the need to get buzzed, Randi got up, walked into her kitchen, and fixed herself a very stiff martini. She could still taste the sweet juices of Roni's pussy in her mouth. It didn't take long for her to realize that Roni was gay and, therefore, the weak link in the GMBs' chain. Randi had been sleeping with the same sex for more than a decade so she knew all the tricks. Once she set her sights on Roni, Roni didn't have a chance. It was because of her sexual preference that her parents had disowned her and kicked her out. If her father wouldn't have come home from work early one day and caught her and her best friend in a compromising position, they may have never found out.

She'd held that grudge against her parents until the days they died and even though they were ready to forgive her, she wasn't ready to forgive them. Hence, the therapy every Friday. She shook her head and thought about how cruel life could be sometimes. The day she was finally ready to let it all go, her father was taken from her.

Once again the buzzing sound of her cell phone jarred her back from her dreadful trip down Memory Lane. She looked at the screen and smiled. *Whatever trouble she got in with Jasmine must didn't amount to too much*, thought Randi, *or she wouldn't be sniffin' up my ass so soon.*

Instead of answering it, she let it go to her voicemail. The best way to hook someone, in her opinion, was to get them so hot for you that they couldn't stand it, and then make them suffer by staying away from them. Randi finished her martini and drifted off to sleep.

$ $ $

Roni woke the next morning with money on her mind. She hated to admit it, but ever since she'd met Randi a couple of nights ago, it seemed that she was going soft and losing her focus. Today, she was going to prove to Jasmine, as well as herself, that she was still a dangerous, cold-blooded, Get Money Bitch and she knew just what she was going to do. By keeping her ear to the streets, she'd heard that the numbers man, Dennis, was going on vacation to the Bahamas that afternoon. It was common knowledge around the way that Dennis didn't trust banks and kept his money hid somewhere. Some people speculated that he had it tucked away in a different location, but Roni didn't believe that for a second. Dennis liked money entirely too much to be too far away from it. A twinge of guilt struck her as she contemplated what she was going to do to Dennis, but she was a GMB so she had to do something to gain back Jasmine's respect. After trying once again, unsuccessfully, to get in touch with Randi, Roni sighed and went into her closet and took out her get-busy tools.

"I might as well be tryin' ta get in touch wit fuckin' Barack Obama," she complained, as she took out masking tape, a blowtorch, and about a yard of rope. She also grabbed her lock-picking tools. Looking at her watch told her that she had to hurry up. Dennis would be leaving in about forty-five minutes. Roni bagged up her tools and headed for the door.

She sped along the inner city streets of Cleveland, disregarding the speed limit, on her way to make a come-up. Once she got to his street, Roni backed into an abandoned duplex that sat directly across the street from where Dennis lived. Looking up and down the streets, she quickly ran into Dennis' backyard. She then pulled out her special tool that she used for breaking and entering.

Disabling the lock was child's play for Roni as she expertly picked it. Dropping down on all fours, Roni slowly crawled into Dennis' living room where he was checking his suitcase. Without warning, Roni sprang up and cracked Dennis in the back of the head with the butt of her .45-caliber pistol. Dennis dropped to the floor like a sack of potatoes.

Roni dragged his semiconscious body into his bedroom and tied him to the bed facedown and spread-eagle. Dennis shook his head, trying to clear the cobwebs, but before he could see her face, she quickly covered his eyes with a blindfold. Then she took a knife out of her back pocket and cut off his pants.

When Dennis finally came back around, he couldn't see a thing through the black rag obstructing his sight. Roni was up on him so fast that he also didn't know who had hit him.

"Who the fuck is that?" he asked after he heard noises.

"Nigga, don't fuckin' worry 'bout it! All you need to worry 'bout is tellin' me where the fuck yo numbers stash is!"

"Numbers stash? What numbers stash?" he said like he didn't know what she was talking about.

"Muthafucka, don't play wit' me! Now I'ma ask yo' ass one more time and only one more time! Where the fuck is the money?"

"Sweetheart, youz 'bout to be a disappointed bitch 'cause I ain't got no muthafuckin' stash!"

Roni looked at Dennis' thin, five-foot-seven-inch frame and knew if she tortured him hard enough, he would eventually give up the dough. "Okay, you old-ass son of a bitch! We can do this the hard way!"

Roni walked over to Dennis' stereo system, turned it on, and pumped up the volume so that no one could hear him scream. Then she reached into her bag and took out the blowtorch. After turning it on and setting fire to the tip, she looked down at Dennis, who was now straining his ears to hear what was going on. She leaned down and whispered in his ear.

"You sure you don't wanna tell me where the money is, muthafucka? This is yo' last muthafuckin' chance!"

"I told you before, bitch, I ain't got no fuckin' money!" he tried to yell over the music.

Roni knew that was a lie. Dennis had been running numbers for the better part of thirty years and was a notorious cheapskate. Roni slowly eased the torch up Dennis' inner thigh.

"Fuck!" Dennis screamed as he squirmed, trying to get away from the intense heat. "Ah shit! I'ma kill yo' ass when I get loose, bitch!"

Ignoring his empty threats, Roni held the torch in one spot and watched Dennis' flesh burn. Dennis yanked and pulled with all his might, but Roni had the rope so tight that it was close to cutting his skin.

"Where the dough at, muthafucka?"

"Fuck you, bitch!"

"Oh, I see you wanna be one of dem tough muthafuckas, huh?"

Roni pushed the flame up between Dennis' legs and let the flame rest on his nuts. It took less than five seconds for him to submit. "Ah shit! OKAY! OKAY! The safe is in the closet! It's in the closet!"

Roni pulled the handheld torch from beneath Dennis' legs and set it down. Then she walked over to the closet, opened the door, and spotted the safe off to the right. "What's the fuckin' numbers, nigga?"

When Dennis took a little too long to answer, Roni calmly walked back over to the torch, picked it up, and pushed it toward his testicles again. The hot flame had barely touched his skin when he started yelling out the combination.

Roni opened up the safe and smiled when she saw the stacks and stacks of bills laid neatly in the safe. She strongly suspected that he had more money than that in the house, but this would do... for now. After loading the blue duffle bag with the cash, Roni grabbed a pillow off of Dennis' bed.

"I got some good news for you, D! I'ma let yo' ass go!"

Dennis breathed a sigh of relief, believing that he would make it out of this nightmare alive. His moment was short-lived as Roni finished her statement by saying, "To hell!"

She laughed as she put the pillow to the back of his head and pulled the trigger.

8

Roni zipped down Buckeye Avenue on her way to Jasmine's house. She couldn't wait to show her the dough from the lick she'd pulled. If this didn't show Jasmine that she was still a down-ass Get Money Bitch, nothing would. The last thing she wanted was to get kicked out of the crew. She had no doubt that she could make it on her own, but she looked up to Jasmine and didn't want to disappoint her. With a fifth of Absolut Vodka in her right hand and the bag of money sitting on the passenger seat beside her, Roni made a right onto Jasmine's street and almost made roadkill out of a pregnant woman crossing the street.

"Bitch, get yo' knocked-up ass outta the way!" Roni yelled at the woman.

The woman stuck her middle finger up at Roni and kept it moving. Normally, when a bitch disrespected Roni like that, she would stomp a mudhole in her ass, but she was in such a good mood from her heist that she let it slide. She took another swig of vodka and pulled into Jasmine's driveway. She grabbed the bag of cash and hopped out of the car.

When Jasmine peered out of the window and saw that it was Roni, she frowned. She was still salty at Roni for almost fucking up the job the day before. Nevertheless, she opened the door and allowed her friend to come in. Roni walked through the door with a big smile on her face.

"The fuck yo' ass want?" Jasmine asked as she sat back down on the couch.

Roni followed her and sat on the couch beside her. "J, I know I been fuckin' up lately, but—"

"Yeah, ever since yo' ass been sniffin' Randi's pussy, yo' fuckin' head's been in the clouds."

Just the mention of Randi's name got Roni's pussy jumping, but she couldn't show that in front of Jasmine. "Well," she said, ignoring the comment, "I did somethin' today to show you that I'm still a down-ass Get Money Bitch."

Roni opened the bag and revealed the bundles of cash that were strewn throughout the bag.

"Got damn, Roni; there's gotta be over a hundred thousand dollars there! Where the fuck did you get this shit from?"

"Let's just say a bitch hit the number today," Roni said with a smirk on her face.

A smile slowly crept across Jasmine's face. Rubbing her hands together greedily, she looked at Roni. "Now this is what the fuck I'm talking about. Start counting this shit up while I go make a phone call right quick."

Roni thought it was odd that she wanted to leave the room to make a phone call, but she shrugged her shoulders and started counting.

$ $ $

"Don't answer that fuckin' phone!" Kita's lover yelled.

"But it could be important," Kita purred, the sensation of a wet tongue tickling her clit.

"Fuck that shit, bitch! I'm what's muthafuckin' important!"

Kita arched her back and moaned softly as Melissa's husband's tongue penetrated her cum box. Unbeknownst to both Kita and

Jasmine, Tony was screwing both of them. He told Kita that his name was Patrick in case Jasmine and Kita ever discussed their sex lives with each other.

"You ready, baby? You ready for this dick?"

"Hell yeah, baby! Gimme every inch of that chocolate thunder!"

He politely obliged as he drove his nut ejector deep inside the walls of her pussy. Their rhythm increased as Kita wrapped her legs around his back and crossed her ankles. Kita managed to cum twice before he pulled out and squirted on her stomach.

"Oh shit, baby; that shit felt good as fuck," he said in between breaths. Completely spent, he tried to fall back onto the pillow and fall asleep.

"Oh hell naw, nigga, you better get yo' ass up and go in there and wash yo' ass."

Reluctantly, he slow-walked into the bathroom and hopped in the shower.

While he was getting himself cleaned up, his cell phone rang. Kita couldn't help herself as she picked up the phone and glanced at the screen. Her jaw dropped and her eyes almost popped out of her head when she saw Jasmine's name appear.

"Oh no, the fuck this muthafucka ain't," she said quietly, but with much attitude. She snatched the phone off the nightstand and promptly pressed *talk*.

"Hello," she cautiously said, praying that it was another Jasmine and not her friend. Her hopes were dashed when Jasmine recognized her voice and called her name.

"Kita? What the fuck you doing answering Tony's phone?"

"Tony?" Kita replied. "That muthafucka told me that his name was Patrick."

"Oh hell naw!" Jasmine screamed. "This punk-ass nigga tryin' ta play us!"

An awkward silence fell over the conversation for a few seconds before Jasmine said, "How you feel about this muthafucka? You ain't in love or no bullshit like that, is you?"

"Fuck naw. This muthafucka just a piece of dick to me." Kita attempted to talk low so that Tony couldn't hear her.

"Good, 'cause I want you to blow his fuckin' brains out for even trying to disrespect the GMBs."

Kita hung up, grabbed her .25 out of her nightstand drawer and headed for the bathroom.

$ $ $

Roni drove home on Cloud Nine. Not only did her jack move net the GBMs a cool hundred fifteen thousand dollars, it had put her back in favor with Jasmine. Although she was less than thrilled when Jasmine reminded her of the rule that any heist pulled by a single member of the crew still had to be split with the rest of the crew, she quickly brushed it off. She couldn't help but notice that Jasmine's mood had changed when she returned from making her phone call. Making a mental note to ask her about it later, Roni took another long swig from her bottle of vodka. The liquor had her extremely horny and visions of licking Randi's ass popped into her head. Right on cue, her cell phone rang.

"Hello."

"Hey, baby," Randi said in a sultry voice.

"Don't 'hey, baby' me! I been trying to call yo' ass for the past twenty-four hours! And you know you got my ass in trouble with my girls!" Roni yelled, trying to sound tough.

"Well, excuse the fuck outta me," Randi said, playing along. She knew right off the bat that Roni was trying to act hard. She decided to put her in her place. "I thought that you was yo' own woman, but I see that you ain't. Maybe I should find me a real fuckin' woman then! Peace, bitch!"

Just as Randi knew she would, Roni stopped her. "Wait, baby," Roni said apologetically. "You ain't gotta take the shit to dat extreme."

"You sure? 'Cause I can keep my black ass movin'," she said sassily.

"Come on, baby; you know a bitch didn't mean it that way," Roni said with a twinge of panic in her voice. The vodka she was drinking had her so horny, she was practically foaming at the pussy lips. "Tell you what, baby," she said, starting to slur her words. "Meet me at my place in about thirty minutes and let me make it up to you."

"Damn right you will," Randi sexily said before hanging up in Roni's face.

Pumped with excitement, Roni sped home quickly. She hopped out of her whip, ran into the house, up the stairs, and into the shower. While cleansing her body, Roni couldn't help but smile thinking about Randi. The way Randi made her body feel had her in the sexual twilight zone. No sooner than she had exited the shower and slapped some lotion on her frame, Randi was knocking at the door. Roni walked downstairs, dressed in red stilettos and a matching red thong. When she opened the door, Randi stood there wearing a black trench coat, large sunglasses, and a red wig.

"I heard someone at this address wants to get their pussy eaten," Randi said. Her nasty words caused Roni's pussy to drip.

"You heard right, baby. Bring yo' sexy ass on here, bitch."

Randi smiled wickedly as she walked past Roni, slinging her juicy ass from side to side. Roni, now starting to feel the full effects of the vodka, quickly strolled up behind Randi and wrapped her arms around her, gently squeezing her tits.

"Damn! I can't wait to get these in my mouth," she said greedily.

"Let's have a drink first, baby," Randi said. "I'm thirsty as hell."

Roni didn't know if Randi would be willing to drink the vodka straight like she had been doing, so she went off to the kitchen to get a couple of ice-filled glasses half-filled with cranberry juice. When she came back, Randi asked her if she had any blunts.

"Yeah, I got a couple in the bedroom. Be right back, baby."

As soon as Roni left, Randi slipped a crushed up e-pill into her glass. Then she poured both of them drinks, making sure that Roni got the tainted one. She took out the mini-recorder that she had brought with her and pressed *record*. Looking at her watch, Randi saw that she had three hours to execute her plan. When Roni came back in the room, the two women drank and smoked weed for the next thirty minutes. With Roni half-drunk and high as a kite, Randi started asking her questions about her crew. In true drunk fashion, Roni started telling Randi any and everything she wanted to know about their operation. If she couldn't take the GMBs out, she would take them down, but either way they were gonna pay dearly for the pain they'd caused her.

9

After once again blowing Roni's mind with spine-tingling sex, Randi sat in her whip down the street from Roni's house waiting for her to come out. She knew from Roni running her drunken mouth earlier that she had to be at Jasmine's by seven, which is why she made it a point to set Roni's alarm clock for her. This was going to be it. Her best chance to take down the GMBs. She dialed her accomplice's cell number and told her that the plan was almost ready to be completed. "She's comin' out of the house now. I'm gonna follow her and call you when I get there," she told the person on the other end.

Randi pulled out into the flow of traffic and stayed two car lengths behind Roni. In her alcohol-impaired state, Roni's senses weren't as sharp as they usually were. As she weaved her way through the muddled Cleveland traffic, Randi prayed that Roni didn't get stopped because of her erratic driving.

When Roni got to Jasmine's place and pulled in the driveway, Randi continued driving past the house. When she got to the corner, she made a U-turn and parked. Jasmine's house was about seven houses from the corner.

With an evil grin on her face, Randi called her house and waited for her voicemail to come on. When it did, she pressed *play* on her recorder and put her cell phone on speaker so that her voicemail would have Roni admitting to the crimes that the GMBs were committing. After that she called her accomplice and gave her Jasmine's address. "Oh and just in case something happens to me, there's a recording on my voicemail that incriminates all three of them hoes. The code is nine-six-nine-three."

Randi ended the conversation, grabbed her .380 semiautomatic pistol from her glove compartment, got out of her car, and walked toward Jasmine's place.

$ $ $

"Now that's what the fuck I'm talkin' 'bout!" yelled Kita as she high-fived Roni. "Get Money Bitch!"

"Oh, so now I'm ya girl again, huh?"

"You neva stopped being my fuckin' girl. I just wanted you to get yo' damn priorities straight," Kita said as she counted her cut of the money that Roni had jacked from Dennis.

"I hope you two hoes ain't in here arguing 'cause I really don't feel like hearing that bullshit," Jasmine said as she walked into the room. In her hands she held three glasses and a bottle of Jose Cuervo Margarita.

Then she went back into the kitchen and grabbed two boxes of pizza and brought them back into the living room. The three women sat, devouring the pizzas, and talking shit amongst one another.

"Ahight, enough bullshitin'," Jasmine finally said. "Let's get down to business. Roni, I was telling Kita before you got here about a job I got lined up."

Jasmine smiled wickedly as she outlined in detail how she planned to set up a meeting with her high-priced lawyer. She was at her scandalous best as she shared how she planned on robbing her, killing her, and incinerating her body. Roni and Kita listened intently as Jasmine told them that the job would net them about eighty thousand dollars apiece. Just from her conversations with Melissa, she knew her lawyer was crazy paid. All three women reached for their guns as a knock on the door startled them.

"Get that," Jasmine ordered to Kita.

Kita looked through the peephole, snapped her head around to Roni, and rolled her eyes.

"Ah hell naw! The fuck this bitch doing here?" she yelled, looking at Roni.

Seeing the angry look on Kita's face and the confused look on Roni's, Jasmine took charge like a true leader. She walked over to the door, looked through the peephole, frowned, and cut her eyes at Roni.

"What?" asked a still confused Roni.

When Jasmine opened the door, Randi walked past her like she owned the place. Roni's heart sank.

"Bitch, I know you didn't just walk the fuck in my house like dat!"

"Well, well, well," Randi said, ignoring Jasmine's comment. "If it ain't three the hard way," she said, gazing from one to the other.

"The name is Get Money Bitches, slut! And since yo ass is intruding on our meeting, you need to get the fuck out!"

Before Jasmine could say another word, Randi pulled out her recorder and pressed *play*. Roni was shocked as her drunken voice poured through the device, letting Jasmine and Kita know that she had divulged their business to her lover.

"What the fuck? How the fuck you gonna tell this bitch about our operation?" Jasmine stared at Roni, shaking her head. She was too disgusted to even talk to her. "The fuck you want from us, bitch?" Jasmine spat.

"I want in. What the fuck you think I want?"

Roni sat there with her head down, teary-eyed. She couldn't believe that her lover had played her.

"Now I know you hoes probably wanna talk this shit ova so y'all can just take y'all dumb asses in the back and I'll be waitin' out here." Randi hoped that they would take the bait and leave the room so the final phase of her plan could be ignited.

"And in case you bitches go back there and talk about killing a bitch, this recording is on my home voicemail for a friend of mine to turn into the police if somethin' happens to me."

The three women turned and headed for the kitchen.

"Oh, by the way, Jasmine," she said as she reached into her inside coat pocket. "You like my red wig?"

It was at that instant Jasmine remembered where she had seen Randi before. She was the woman with the red hair that Jasmine spotted in the courtroom the day of her trial. Still slightly confused by it all, she led her crew to the kitchen to talk.

When they came back into the living room to tell Randi that they would accept her offer and include her, they stopped dead in their tracks. Standing next to Randi and holding a .357 Magnum was Melissa.

"What the fuck goin' on in this muthafucka?" Jasmine asked.

"Payback, bitch," Melissa replied. "How long did you two hoes think you were gonna keep fuckin' my husband and I wasn't gonna find out about it? I guess you tramps never realized that he talks in his fuckin' sleep. I've known about you two bitches all along."

"Wait, hol' up." Kita threw her hands up. "Who the fuck is you?"

"She's my lawyer," Jasmine said, answering before Melissa could. "And we've been fuckin' her husband."

"Who, Patrick?"

Melissa snorted out a laugh. "His name is Tony, you stupid hoe," Melissa scolded.

"I hate a dumb bitch," Randi chimed in. Randi then glanced toward Roni, whose eyes were glistening. "Ahhh, don't be sad, boo. It was fun while it lasted."

Instantly getting angry at the thought of being made a fool of, Roni took a step in Randi's direction but stopped cold when Randi pulled a pistol from the small of her back.

"Bitch, you betta ease yo' pussywhipped ass the fuck back!"

"What the fuck you got to do wit any o' this shit?" Kita yelled.

"Oh, I wouldn't have a fuckin' thing to do wit it... if you and yo bitch-ass crew hadn't murdered my parents!"

The GMBs looked at each other and then back at Randi before it finally kicked in.

"Oh shit," said a surprised Jasmine. "That's why yo' ass was in court that day!"

"Yeah, bitch! And lucky for me that your lawyer used her connections to find out who I was so we could get revenge on you bitches!"

"And before you hoes think about trying to rattle me by telling me that my husband is dead, I already know about it." Melissa laughed. "I followed that punk-ass nigga to your house and waited outside for you to leave. You killing him just saved me the trouble of doing it and having to cover it up. As soon as you left, I went inside and spit on his no-good ass. I did play the naïve, hurt wife good, though," she said, patting herself on the back.

Jasmine's mind raced a mile a minute as she tried to think of a way to get to her .38 that was lying under a pillow on the couch. Roni had her pistol in the small of her back but was too heartbroken to think about reaching for it. Kita had left hers in the kitchen but knew if she made a sudden dash for it, she would be rewarded with a bullet in the back. But from where she was standing, she could easily grab Roni's. Knowing that was probably their only chance, she made her move. Melissa and Randi high-fived each other, causing a slight distraction. That was all the time Kita needed as she snatched Roni's gun from her lower back and aimed it at Randi. Acting on pure lover's instinct, Roni screamed at the top of her lungs. "NOOO! DON'T SHOOT HER!"

Just before Kita let off a shot toward Randi, Roni pushed her arm, causing the shot to go wild.

Pow! Kita's body hit the floor with a resounding thud as a bullet from Randi's .380 ripped through her chest.

Jasmine was in total shock. She couldn't believe that Roni had caused the shooting of their friend over a bitch she had just met.

As Kita lay on the floor bleeding profusely and gasping for air, Randi walked over to her and kissed Roni on the lips. "Thanks, baby," she said as she shot Kita in the throat.

Coming out of her shocked state, Jasmine grabbed Roni around the neck and tried to choke the life out of her. "You stupid bitch! What the fuck is wrong with you? You got our best friend killed over this bitch?"

Heat suddenly seared through Jasmine's back as Melissa put two hot slugs into the small of her back. Life drained out of her body as she slumped to the floor. Roni took one look at her two dead best friends and lost it, screaming and crying.

Pow! Pow!

"Bitch, shut up all that damn noise," Randi said as she dumped two shots into Roni's forehead.

"Now," Melissa said. "Where did motor mouth over there say that Jasmine kept her cash?"

Randi ran to the back and checked each room until she came to

Jasmine's. Then she looked up under the bed and pulled out a large black trunk. She dragged it back into the living room and shot the lock off of it. When she opened it, both of their mouths fell open.

"This bitch been stackin' all kinda paper," Melissa said of the trunk loaded with hundreds and fifties. "It's gotta be a half a million in there."

Melissa then walked over to the door where she had dropped two duffle bags down on the floor. "Let's bag this shit up and get the fuck outta here. Grab two of them glasses and that wine, too."

After bagging up the money, the two women cracked the door and peered outside. Cars were passing by, but there was no one standing around so they hurried to Melissa's Lexus SUV, popped the hatch, threw the money inside, and pulled off.

10

After stopping at a convenience store and having Randi run in for a couple of blunts, Melissa drove down to the lake so they could chill out and celebrate. She pulled up close to the edge of the water and cut the car off. "That's what the fuck I'm talking about! We got paid and we got our revenge all at the same muthafuckin' time! You know what? Go back there and get two hundred-dollar bills outta that bag. I got an idea."

While Randi was getting the money, Melissa poured both of them a glass of wine and set them in the cup holders. When Randi got back inside the truck, Melissa took a lighter out of her pocket. "Let me get one o' them blunts you rolled up on the way over here." Melissa then flicked the lighter and lit both bills. She then lit her blunt with the burning money, hoping Randi would follow suit, which she did.

"Look, Randi, I know that this money doesn't make up for your parents not being here, but we did get our revenge," Melissa said, noticing that Randi hadn't spoken since they'd left Jasmine's house. "Let's have a victory toast."

The two women picked up the glasses, clicked them together and downed the wine. Five minutes later, Randi got out and walked around. Melissa looked in the side-view mirror just in time to see Randi collapse to the ground. The boric acid that she had poured in Randi's wine while she was getting the money had done its job.

Melissa puffed on the blunt twice and blew smoke into the air. "I don't split money or niggas with bitches," she said, driving off. She smiled as she looked in the mirror. "Get money, bitch," she said to herself. "Get money."

C.J. Hudson grew up in the inner city of Cleveland, Ohio. He witnessed firsthand what it was like to be around murderers, crack dealers, and thieves. Refusing to become another statistic, C.J. attended Kent State University after graduating from East High School. Years later he enrolled at Kaplan Institute, where he received his certificate in electricity. An avid reader for over eighteen years, C.J. signed with Life Changing Books in 2009 and penned his first novel, Chedda Boyz, *in 2010. Since then he has penned* Next Door Nympho, *also published by LCB, and has self-published* Mo Chedda, *the sequel to* Chedda Boyz, *and an ebook entitled* Hood Luv. *He is currently hard at work on his next project. Visit the author at www.authorcjhudson.com*

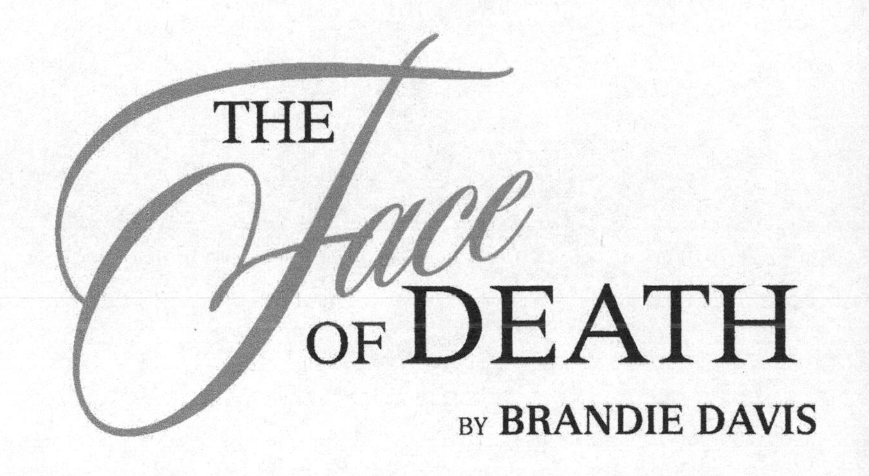

THE *Face* OF DEATH

BY BRANDIE DAVIS

1

"How much would you guess each tit is worth?"

"A quarter of a million."

The blue-eyed plastic surgeon looked over at his partner. "I said guess."

"There's no need to; I can feel the worth of each tit just by holding it in my hand."

Harvey extracted the implant filled with liquid heroin out of the twenty-three-year-old mule's right breast and held it in his palm. Blood painted his latex gloves ruby red and glistened in the brightly lit operating room. Groping the implant with his fingers, he took a whiff of it, allowed his tongue to retreat out of his mouth, and licked a portion of it until it was stain free.

"A quarter of a million more reasons men will be addicted to these. Isn't life grand?"

The taste and feel of an implant pulled Harvey into a world of ecstasy. There was nothing he was more infatuated with than a set of fake breasts. Smith and four other doctors hired to remove heroin-filled implants from out of Colombian women's bodies stopped what they were doing and watched the obscene act. They all knew of Harvey's addiction but never had they seen it with their own two eyes. Smith turned away from the scene and his vision fell on Bobbi.

She was standing behind the glass window in the comfort of the dimly lit observation room watching Harvey's every move. Her bloodshot eyes shot daggers into Harvey's back, and curly locks the color of mocha, covered her cheeks. Her large hair made her head appear to be drastically small. Seconds passed and Bobbi's eyes met Smith's. Immediately he turned away and focused on what he'd forgotten was important—retrieving her heroin.

The intercom came alive and Bobbi's voice filled the room.

"Harvey, keep fucking with my product and I'm going to send you to Colombia and have them stuff your balls with that shit."

Harvey fondled the implant a little more and then dropped it into the tin pan. "I'm sorry. Sometimes I get a little carried away and can't help myself. Maybe if you let me play with yours sometimes, Bobbi, we wouldn't have this problem." Looking over his shoulder, his wrinkled skin stretched, and Bobbi's silhouette filled the corner of his eye.

Bobbi shook her head. She didn't understand Harvey's fetish, but she did understand that she needed him. He and Smith were two of the top plastic surgeons in America and she needed them to train the new doctors she brought onboard to be just as good as them. Business had taken off and the two of them could no longer handle the workload coming their way. Colombian women engulfed in the drug world were running at the chance to smuggle heroin into the U.S. through their breast implants. They all wanted the opportunity to have an upscale, free boob job performed by America's best once the drug was removed. For women obsessed with vanity, quality implants were hard to come by in the land of the poor, so when free was thrown in their face, they all ran to catch it, regardless of the consequences.

"You wouldn't want to; mine are real."

Harvey nodded his head and placed his attention back on the task at hand.

"Okay, ladies, let's stop fooling around and touch some more jugs! I don't want to see any scars! We're in the business of making this shit look as natural as possible!" he told the men in scrubs. And just like that, the professional super surgeon with a waiting list of women wanting him to revamp their breasts was back. The imagery of real breasts sickened him and immediately he retreated back to a world of silicone and saline breasts. Bobbi grinned. Harvey was like every other man she stumbled upon. The second things got real, he got ghost. She pushed the round white button plastered on the wall and the high-tech observation room lit up. Beethoven's "Moonlight Sonata" blared through the speakers and the curtains closed, giving Bobbi and her workers their much needed privacy.

Sitting on the leather couch, Bobbi removed a small bag of cocaine from her purse and emptied its contents on the coffee table. She divided it into four thin lines and with a hunch of her back, cleaned the table dry. Within minutes, the drug had entered her system and all was well. Her head moved to Beethoven's piano and in that moment, life was the way it used to be, and should have been, until the day she died.

Images of happiness plagued her vision and sent tears jumping to their death, but her head wouldn't stop moving; instead it moved faster and on beat with the dark, chilling song. Stuck in a world of bliss and depression, past thoughts crept into her mind. Bobbi never understood men's obsession with women and why they had to have several women when they had one whose qualities made up the perfect woman. Her fingers danced in the air, pretending to play the piano when her right hand grazed the oxford fabric curtains. The feel of the material pulled her out of her zone and forced her to peek inside the operating room. She watched as each man handled each patient's breasts so delicately, anyone would have mistaken it for love, but Bobbi knew the truth. There was no one that could tell her once the pieces were put together and their bride of Frankenstein was brought to life, they wouldn't treat her like shit and discard her for another pair of breasts that came their way. Women were nothing but knick-knacks men collected and set along their windowsill so they could admire their conquests.

Bobbi slammed her back against the couch and allowed a river of tears to flow down her dark-chocolate cheeks. This is why she stopped watching the surgeries. Like these women, she had been reconstructed and made into what a man desired. They were a reminder that her significant other was reasonable for crowning her queen of the underworld and granting her the East Coast to reign. He killed who she once was and in its place created a monster; there was no coming back for her, because now she was too comfortable to go back in time. He made her into his life-sized horror Barbie and shortly after, fell into the beds of countless women. His betrayal opened up a door inside of Bobbi she never knew existed and didn't wish to close. The pain, which circulated through her veins, was indescribable and suffocating. Each day she woke up with an ounce more of rage and a conscience full of anger. But this was the life she chose; therefore every day she told herself that this would be the life she led.

Wiping away her tears with the tips of her fingers, Bobbi laughed at her weakness. *In time I'll feel nothing and pain will be but a figment of my imagination.* Getting herself together, she stood up and slammed her hand against the white button. Instantly the curtains opened and her bread and butter were once again revealed to her. A soft, soothing smile spread across her face, and a sense of ease took over her. "Keep doing what you're doing, Bobbi," she told herself. "Keep doing what you're doing."

2

Two hours later, all three pairs of implants were removed and replaced with silicone breasts that filled the mules' chests. Bobbi watched the entire procedure and not once did she move from where she stood. The human body was a beautiful thing and it amazed her how much it could take without giving out. From time to time, flashbacks blocked her vision, but she pushed them away and watched her men dehumanize the Colombian women. Once upon a time when she was in her natural state of mind, she yearned to be a plastic surgeon. The art of it all stimulated her senses and caused her to come alive. She once viewed the human body as a block of clay, and her hands the sculptor, but now, it was her moneymaker. Her passion for medicine died a long time ago when she was forced into a new world and turned her into a new person.

"Another beautiful, big-busted woman now walks the earth. Where is my trophy for the fine work I have performed?" Harvey walked inside the observation room, his eyes fixated on Bobbi while removing his scrubs. "You're not answering me so I assume that means I get no trophy. So how about a kiss?"

"What do you want?" Bobbi hissed, irritation pulsating throughout her tone.

"What I want you won't tell me, not even if I begged." He threw his soiled scrubs on the couch and stood beside her, his hands clasped behind his back.

Bobbi observed the cleaning ladies work their magic. Within minutes, the operating room was almost spotless. "Try me."

Any trace of humor evaporated and was replaced with attentiveness.

"You lied about your breasts being real, why?"

Bobbi turned in Harvey's direction. "What are you talking about?"

"You told me your breasts are real, when you and I both know that's a lie. But instead of me coming to my own conclusions, I'd rather ask why you would lie in the first place." Harvey's eyes burned holes into Bobbi's overly worked-on face. An uneasy feeling came over her and instantly she became defensive.

"Because it's none of your fucking business. You're hired to recover my shit, not to ask questions."

Harvey smirked, a light bulb going off on top of his head.

"Oh, I see." He paused, his mind wandering off for a brief moment. "Take my advice and direct that anger to the person who's responsible for it."

Bobbi's face scrunched up and her body temperature rose. She gritted her teeth, inhaled and exhaled like she was in Lamaze class.

"I'ma ask you one more time; what the fuck are you talking about?"

"I've been a surgeon for over twenty years. I can tell when a woman's had work done, and because I'm a man, I can tell when a woman's hurt over doing something for someone other than herself."

Silence slammed into the room and Bobbi felt like the wind had been knocked out of her. This was the first time since she could remember someone actually caring enough to observe her behavior and come to their own conclusion. Her mouth glued shut, with just one lie, he'd read her like a book without skipping any pages.

"What you know doesn't matter; what's done doesn't matter."

"I think it does, because if it didn't, you would be numb to it all. You're in a business where one slipup can cost you everything, yet this is the first time in four months since you last showed your face in your own operating room. I bet you hide in here behind the glass and cry yourself a river, don't you? Tell me, do you gloss those high cheekbones of yours with your tears every chance you get? Watching these surgeries is like looking in the mirror, isn't it?"

Bobbi's head pushed back and after one good snort, spat into Harvey's face. Mucus dripped from his nose and fell onto the floor.

"You know nothing about me; you know nothing about how it feels to watch women have a choice over whether or not their appearance is reconstructed while you stand there and look like this." Bobbi's unpolished fingernail directed his attention to her sunken face, permanent eyebrows, and high cheekbones. But even though she pointed to the multiple works done on her face, he couldn't take his focus off the scar stretched across her throat. "They come to us to make them beautiful and cut into their skin; we don't force them. *They* have a choice, but *I* didn't. I wish all I got was a fucking boob job."

Harvey maneuvered his way toward the corner of the room and retrieved a tissue from its box that sat comfortably on its wooden stand and wiped off her bodily fluids.

"You're right, I don't know how it feels, but I do know you're too beautiful to hold on to the past."

"Beautiful? Do you see who you're talking to?" Bobbi's once normal-sized forehead wrinkled. Her last job had altered her hairline and made it significantly smaller.

Harvey walked across the room where a waist-length mirror hung from a nail.

"Come here," he instructed.

Bobbi hesitated. She stood clear of her kryptonite, known as mirrors. It was the cat to her mouse that she avoided at all costs. When her boots didn't lift from off the floor, he encouraged her once more to come his way. Buying herself some time, Bobbi activated the curtains to shut, and watched them separate herself from the room. Her legs felt like cement and for a brief moment, she stared at the fabric, preparing herself for what she was about to see. She put on a brave face and slowly walked in Harvey's direction. When she reached him, Harvey moved out of her way and allowed her to stand in front of him. Bobbi's head dropped, refusing to look at her own reflection.

From behind, he reached around her and touched her chin. She flinched; no one had touched her face since her last surgery. But instead of her sudden movement startling him, he lifted her face up to the glass. They stood in that position for minutes at a time, when finally her eyes fell on the mirror. She took in her appearance. Her first reaction was to turn away, but the longer she looked, the easier it got. Her skin was tight and shiny, her lips thin, and her cheekbones high; she was beautifully ugly. The only thing she recognized about herself was her nose and eyes; everything else was completely foreign. She turned her head to the side and viewed herself from a different angle. She stared at her reflection straight on. Her eyes eventually dropped to the scar on her neck. Her fingers began to trace its outline.

"How did that happen?"

Bobbi's eyes bounced over to Harvey's reflection. She completely forgot he was still standing behind her.

"I tried to kill myself."

Harvey's eyes locked on hers. He was not expecting that response. He wanted to ask why, but the question seemed too personal, even for him. But Bobbi sensed his curiosity and awarded him his satisfaction.

"I couldn't stand how I looked after the surgeries. I just wanted it all to end. Every time I thought he was done using my face as a canvas, another surgery was scheduled. I was tired of it."

Harvey suddenly grew quiet. There were times when all a person needed to do was listen; sometimes an ear was mightier than the mouth.

"I don't know why I tried to slit my own throat. At the time, I was so enraged and willing to do anything just to stop the pain." She looked at the scar a little harder. "Every surgery that rolled around, I told myself I would stand up to him and tell him no, but I never did. He's not someone you can talk up against."

Harvey moved his hand from her chin and allowed it to plummet down to her neck. He pushed her hand away and began caressing the scar. Bobbi's eyes widened. She never imagined anyone ever wanting to touch it; normally she would receive looks of fear or sympathy from strangers walking by. Its unattractiveness created a force field around her entire being that no one wanted to puncture, until now. Frozen in shock, Bobbi watched as Harvey rubbed and poked at the scar. Right as she was beginning to feel comfortable with him touching the keloid, his hand slithered down to her breasts, his free hand seconds behind the first. Her heart raced and throat instantly became parched. She had no idea how to react; a man hadn't touched her in months, so the sudden change in routine threw her off course. Her hand flew up and pushed his away.

"I can't," she said softly.

Harvey wrapped his arms around her slim waist. "He will never find out. For once, do what you want."

Bobbi's heart skipped a beat. In the past five years, she never did what she wanted. Whatever her partner told her to do, she did without question. He ruled with fear and the last thing she wanted to do was be on the receiving end of his anger. Fear was the reason she allowed him to take her soul and outer appearance away. It was hard telling the king of the West no to anything he wanted, so now she stood, a shell of her former self, a figment of her own imagination. But to hear someone encourage her to do something for herself was enticing, and to do the unthinkable with Harvey would be spellbinding. Twenty years her senior and of Caucasian descent made them opposites, but she wanted him and he wanted her from the first day he laid eyes on her. They were both odd, both weird and unexplainable, but together they worked. Together they not only made magic, but sense. All she had to do was cross-over and step back into a world where a hint of normalcy was present. However, that was always easier said than done.

"He'll find out," she whispered.

"It'll be pretty hard for him to suspect a fifty-year-old white man of sleeping with his wife while he's on the West Coast, don't you think?"

Bobbi grabbed his hand and held it in hers. "That's the reason why he did this to me." Harvey's eyebrows rose in confusion. "He needed someone he could control and trust to run the East while he took care of things on the West, but he didn't think he could do that without first devaluing me." Her left hand touched her face. "It's hard for a woman to cheat when she looks like this. He calls it his form of insurance."

Uncontrollable tears raced down her cheeks; every day she asked herself how could she allow him to wash away who she was, but every time that question dashed through her mind, she gave the same answer. *It's hard to say no to someone who murdered for less than fifty dollars.*

"Take a leap of faith. We've always wanted this, but now we need this. I know you want me as much as I want you." Harvey's hands found their way back on her breasts. "I like every fake thing about you, down to the little bit of veracity you have left."

Terror found its way back into Bobbi's heart. The thought of Ruben finding out about her infidelity caused her body to shut down. But the sound of her stepping out of the norm, breaking the rules and doing something that she wanted for once, was alluring. She was tired of being lonely and running an empire while her king degraded and broke each and every one of their vows while away for months at a time. Life was hard, but she was ready to make it easier.

Turning around, she looked at Harvey, and for one minute said nothing. She needed him to understand that what she was about to commit to was not to be taken lightly.

"We do this my way, but promise me when you love me, you'll love me hard." She batted her eyelashes, her need for affection shining through.

"I'll do you one better. I'll love you like a pair of silicone implants, always and forever."

Bobbi smiled.

"But first something must be done."

Bobbi's head fell forward, afraid of what may slip out from his mouth.

"I need you to do a few more surgeries."

Bobbi pulled from his hold and faced him. Her eyes were filled with pain and outlined with fury.

"This is what this is all about; I'm nothing but a project to you? You want to see if you can fix my face!"

Bobbi stormed past him and headed straight for the door; her destination was the office bathroom. She thought she was going to be sick. She actually believed that he might have loved her.

Harvey raced after her and grabbed her arm. "What this is, is me trying to make you happy! If it were up to me, I would have you any way, but you deserve to be happy in your skin."

Like a flowing river, tears raced down Bobbi's face. In her world this was anything but normal. This was nonexistent. They were two weirdos sharing normal love, a love they both tried to avoid since day one, but now that he was putting all his cards out on the table, hiding was no longer an option. She took a deep breath, realizing that the only way out of her skin was to take the journey through.

"What will we have to do?"

"We fix what he's done to you, but first," his hand landed on her neck, "we get rid of this."

Bobbi nodded her head in total agreement. "Then there is where we start."

3

One Month Later

Standing in the hospital's hallway, Bobbi peered inside the nursery. On the other side of the large glass window was a room full of newborns. Innocence enveloped the room and for a brief moment sent her back in time to when her life wasn't riddled with hate and resentment. Standing beside her were strangers from seemingly all walks of life, admiring the new additions to their families. Ronald McDonald smiles adorned their faces and forced Bobbi's frown to stand out. Her husband's newborn was gorgeous. Her chocolate skin glowed and big brown eyes resembled her own. Even she found it hard to believe that it hadn't been her legs stationed on those stirrups.

Her dark shades concealed her face while her black leather jacket and combat boots made her resemble a biker. Like always, her curly locks were unruly and stood high around her head. The baby must have felt the negative vibes radiating off of Bobbi because after only sleeping for fifteen minutes, she woke up screaming. Her cries were high-pitched and filled with distress. Witnessing the child struggle for comfort and a nurse rush to her aid, put a smile on Bobbi's face. The moment was priceless.

"You shouldn't be here."

Bobbi's smile dissolved and an emotionless stare took its place.

"We have to go. If Ruben found out you were here, he'd…"

"He'd what?" Bobbi spat, her attention still on the baby. "He'll come from L.A. and kill me? Or would he have you do it instead?" After making the last comment, she looked directly at Levi who stood to her right. His eyes met hers but never did he reveal during their stare-down that the only thing in life he regretted doing was killing Harvey. Like everything else, it was nothing but a job to him. However, when he saw the look in Bobbi's eyes while she hovered over Harvey's blood-drenched body, he knew the bullet he put through Harvey's chest hit Bobbi in the heart and killed her too. That night he demolished a love in desperate need of blossoming and in its place created a dead zone by the name of Bobbi. Killing Harvey and babysitting Bobbi was supposed to be easy. Instead, it turned into the hardest thing Levi ever had to do.

"Let's go, there's nothing here for you," he whispered.

"Nothing here for me? I beg to differ." Her head turned toward the newborn.

"Listen," he whispered. He looked around, assuring no one was listening. "I'll speak to Ruben and see about having them moved out of New York. Sort of like an 'out of sight, out of mind' kinda thing."

Bobbi laughed, her shoulders moving up and down. "That's exactly what I had in mind: out of sight, out of mind."

Levi's neck tightened. He didn't like hearing Bobbi threaten his cousin's family. He grabbed her by the elbow pulling her away from the nursery, but the second he made contact, she looked down at his grip.

"You don't want to do that," she snarled.

Through her blackout shades, he identified a heartless killer. An animal in the form of a human who was ready to attack at any minute. He released his hold of her and fought to calm himself down. It was things like this that confirmed Ruben had no idea who his wife had turned into after the death of Harvey.

"Rue, you told me this would be an easy way to wipe out my brother's debt. Yet you got me babysitting the fuckin' Bonnie to your Clyde over here."

Levi stood in front of his car parked in front of Bobbi's house. She wouldn't let him in, but when he finally used the key supplied by her husband, she welcomed him with a gun to the face. This was week two of him being on the job and if things like this continued, he didn't know what he would do.

"I consider killing my wife's boyfriend and making sure she doesn't fuck another one of her surgeons easy. Especially when in return, you're receiving fifty-thousand dollars. And what the fuck are you talking about—Bonnie? She runs shit over there for me, but she's no killer."

"Let me ask you something, Rue. When was the last time you seen her?"

"It's been a minute, why?"

"Because I'm beginning to think the woman you knew no longer exists. She's cold and if you ask me…lost." Levi looked back at the house. All the lights were off and the darkness of the night masked him from prying eyes. Looking up at Bobbi's window, he sensed her watching him, regardless that her curtains were shut tight.

"What are you trying to say, that I don't know my wife?"

"I'm not saying that at all. I'm just saying that maybe she's not who you thought she was. Maybe killing dude really fucked her up."

Ruben sat up straight on his couch and leaned over, his free hand forcefully pushing the female who was napping on his lap off of him. He adjusted the phone firmly to his ear, confident that Levi would hear everything he had to say.

"I'ma act like I didn't just hear you accuse me of not knowing my wife and her being emotional over another motherfucker, only because you're family. So whatever mood you *think* Bobbi is in, brush it off as her being on her period or some shit, and do your fuckin' job."

The line went dead. Levi's huge hand squeezed the phone until his skin turned red. He jammed it into his pocket. He couldn't stand the way Ruben spoke to him. If it wasn't for his brother's debt, he wouldn't be Ruben's errand boy.

He jumped in his car and didn't hesitate putting the key in the ignition, but the moment he prepared to pull from the curb, something told him to look at the house once more. Again, his eyes landed on Bobbi's window. Her silhouette materialized. Without warning, the tables had turned and Levi was no longer the one watching Bobbi, but the one being watched.

Levi snapped back to reality right in time to witness Bobbi leave. He watched as she slowly walked past him and in the direction of Ruben's mistress' room. He knew he should have stopped her. Controlling Bobbi and assuring her puppet strings remained tight was part of his job description, but he owed it to her to look the other way. Stuck in his thoughts, he never noticed Bobbi had turned around and now stood behind him.

"You work for me...tell me everything you know about Ruben. I want to know about his women and the business he's hidden from me. He took from me; now it's time I take from him. You do so and I will pay off your brother's debt within a matter of days."

Levi didn't look her way; instead his eyes focused on the many people tapping on the glass and admiring their new additions. His silence indicated that she had his full attention.

"But if you don't, your brother dies while all you do is watch."

Levi's eyes jumped around the crowded nursery. No one heard the death threat he was receiving, and no one gave the woman dressed in solid black a second look. The guard nearby socialized with a doctor, never sensing Levi's discomfort. Bobbi calmly walked away, the powerful echo of her boots reinforcing her last words to him.

Thoughts of betrayal bounced around Levi's mind. He should have spat in her face and been confident that if he told his cousin her proposal, he would have been pulled out of this compromising position, but he wasn't so self-assured after all. Telling Ruben would have done nothing but make it look like he needed Ruben once more. When Levi's older brother's gambling got out of hand, he found himself owing a total of fifty-thousand dollars to various people he couldn't pay off. Time was of the essence and with each day that passed, his life was closer to ending. Levi did everything he could to try and scrape up the money, but it was a lost cause that wound up pushing him and his brother to do the one thing they dreaded: go to their cousin for help.

Being Ruben's cousin was never easy. It required patience and a lot of tongue holding. Growing up, the shoe was on the other foot, and Levi and his family were the wealthy ones. Several times Ruben's mother was forced to ask for her sister's help financially, and although the family never minded lending a helping hand, Ruben did. The jester made him feel belittled and needy; however, each time his mother asked for help, his hunger for money grew without boundaries and his determination to outdo his cousins flourished. At the age of twenty-five, the tables had turned, and Levi's family wealth unexpectedly went down the drain. It must have resurfaced in Ruben's pockets because the moment they lost it all, he gained the world. Numerous times the brothers were in need, but after seeing how Ruben behaved once he finally made a buck, the siblings stayed away from acquiring his help.

Ruben waited for the day his cousins would need him, and although it didn't happen right away, he knew one day it would. That one day came one month ago. Standing on his doorstep, Ruben listened to everything his cousins had to say and when they were done speaking, he told them he would help them but under one condition.

"I'll give you the money but not for free."

Levi and McDaniel didn't expect to receive a handout, but they did expect for their cousin to remember all of the money their mother had given him without asking for it back. Each generation that came along was nothing like the one before and Levi was witnessing it firsthand.

"What do you want?" Levi inquired.

"I want you to work for me. It looks like my wife is having an affair, so I want you to take care of that problem, and then watch her for two months. Make sure her head is back in the game. Then, and only then, will I give you the money."

Levi's face wrinkled.

"Hold up, why Levi? I'm the one in debt. I'll be your little errand boy," McDaniel voiced.

"Two months! You won't give us the money until the next two months?" Levi questioned, his tone filled with disgust.

Ruben looked at Levi, but what came out of his mouth was the answer to McDaniel's question. "Because I want to break him."

And there it was, the answer to everyone's assumptions. Ruben hated Levi for some unknown reason.

He turned to Levi and answered his question. "In two months, after everything's done, you'll get your money." And without another word, he stood up and left from out his living room.

McDaniel looked at his brother. He was the oldest, but Levi always took the lead, leaving him to do nothing but follow.

"What do we do?"

Levi didn't want to answer; he was too engulfed in anger. It took all he had not to run behind his cousin and beat some sense into him.

"We do what he says. But while we wait on the money, you can't stay in L.A. You have to hide out somewhere. Somewhere not even he knows about." Levi nodded his head in the direction Ruben left in. Seconds later, he reappeared, taking the seat he occupied prior.

"Deal or no deal?"

Levi faced his cousin and without hesitation answered, "Deal." His guard was laid down and off the strength of his brother, he would do what he had to in order to save his life.

"Great." Ruben stood up. "You start now. If you're going to work for me, there are a few things you should know."

"I don't need to know anything about your business, Ruben," Levi responded.

"Of course you do. You're my cousin and I have a feeling you'll do so well that I'll want you permanently on my payroll. I always wanted you to work for me," Ruben antagonized.

Levi looked into space, semi-listening to everything he said.

"But first we have fun." Ruben smiled and on cue, the doorbell rang. He walked to the entrance and opened it for a group of women clad in tight skirts and heels. Within seconds, a few of them flocked to Levi and McDaniel, their hands exploring their bodies while playing Christopher Columbus. Their laughs filled the air, but all Levi and McDaniel could do was stare at one another and wish they didn't need Ruben.

A toddler ecstatic to see her new baby brother banged on the glass from on top of her uncle's shoulders and shook Levi from his past. He looked in the nursery at the child whose attention the little girl was desperately trying to receive. He smiled. The newborn was a spitting image of his sister. Soon after, Levi's eyes jumped from child to child. Life was different when you weren't aware of the horrors that lay in the world, so in that moment, Levi wished he could trade places with either of those children. His eyes landed on Ruben's firstborn. His face dropped in shame and his leg shook in fear. It wasn't until he was the only one staring at the babies did his hand touch the glass and he told her, "I'm sorry."

He had no choice but to accept Bobbi's offer. She didn't require much, and in some kind of way he would be making up for what he'd done, not to mention she agreed to pay off McDaniel's debt faster than Ruben. Levi looked one last time at the child. He wasn't at all sorry for betraying his cousin, however, he was sorry that he was betraying his new family.

4

Tucked away in a dark corner, Bobbi watched her prey who was in a deep slumber. Her past face stared back at her and reminded her of what used to be. Her heart rate sped up and she practiced maintaining control by pacing her breaths. The figure in bed tossed and turned, her legs kicked, and head moved from side to side, discomfort disturbing her rest. The hospital door opened, blocking Bobbi's view of Robbi. In walked an elderly African American woman who made her way to Robbi's bedside. Observing her restless sleep, she placed her hand on her arm in an effort to calm her down. Robbi's eyes shot open and her body twisted out her reach.

"Who are you!" she shrieked, her head inches off the pillow while her mind fought to make sense of what was taking place.

The nurse smiled, unfazed by her frazzled behavior. "It's okay, sweetheart, you had a bad dream. I'm Nurse Teller." She paused, smiling at Robbi so that she could see she came in peace. But by the look on Robbi's face, it was obvious that she was still wound up and had yet to relax.

"Oh," was the only thing that escaped her mouth. She had given birth over four hours ago and there was still no sign of Ruben. Her head sunk into the pillows and tears tumbled from her eyes. She turned away from Nurse Teller, unwilling to have her see the defeated look splashed across her face.

"I was told you've been complaining about pain due to the C-section. I'm here to give you something and then I'll be on my way."

Agitated that the nurse was still in her presence, Robbi held out her hand without looking her way. "Let's get this over with," she spat. Rushing Nurse Teller to drop the pills in the center of her hand, she wiggled her fingers.

An uneven grin crossed Nurse Teller's lips.

"Oh no, my dear. I have to give you a needle."

Robbi wiped away her tears and turned in the nurse's direction. "Fine, just hurry up. I want to be alone."

Her nasty tone of voice made Nurse Teller proud to give her a needle; it was people like her she liked bringing pain to.

"Sit up, honey, and hold your arm straight out for me."

Robbi did as she was told. Glancing around the room, she felt the nurse prep her for her needle, then finally felt her injecting the meds.

"All done! See, it wasn't that bad."

Robbi didn't respond; she waited for her to clean her wound and cover it with a bandage. When she finished her task, Robbi said one last thing to her.

"Why is this room so dark? Can I get some light in here?"

"Of course, on my way out, I'll turn on the light."

Slowly, Nurse Teller headed for the door, her small hands cutting on all the lights while closing the door behind her. "Goodnight, sweetheart. Now don't scream too loud."

Before Robbi got a chance to respond to her comment, the nurse had closed the door, giving Robbi a clear view of Bobbi.

"What the fuck are you doing here?" It was like seeing a ghost. The last time Robbi saw her sister was months ago. She had been standing with Ruben by her side, telling Bobbi she was pregnant.

"I can't see my sister after she gives birth?"

"Where's Ruben!"

"In L.A. Where else would he be?"

"Don't fuck with me, Bobbi! Where is Ruben? What did you do to him?"

Robbi was sitting upright, her body trembling in fear. It was hard for her to accept that Ruben screwed her over, so instead she blamed it on her twin.

"I have nothing to do with his absence. He abandoned you and that little bastard all on his own."

"Get the fuck out!" she yelled. Tears welled in her eyes. She thought she finally had Ruben all to herself.

"I'll leave when you don't have my husband's child…oops, you already have. So I guess that means I'm not going anywhere." Bobbi leaned over, her elbows positioned on her knees. She cocked her head to the right and the light bounced off the tightness of her left cheek.

"You're so ugly. I wish you succeeded when you tried killing yourself."

Robbi's stunning face was drenched in tears. What she never told her sister was that she missed her—but not in the everyday sense. She missed how she used to be before she met Ruben; she missed her inner beauty and her drive to become a surgeon. Bobbi wasn't the only one who found it hard living in her new skin; her twin suffered, too, with every day that passed.

Robbi's affair with Ruben started when she tried to tear him and Bobbi apart. She wanted her sister to have her life back and the only way she saw that happening was if she seduced her husband and got her from under his thumb, but it didn't work. Not only did Bobbi not leave her husband, but Robbi fell for Ruben. Her entire scheme had changed within the snap of a finger. Long gone was her determination to save her sister. Robbi had now set out to keep her man.

Bobbi's hand flew up to her neck, rubbing the spot where her scar once was. Before Harvey died, he removed the recurring reminder. He never got a chance to work on her face, but he did get a chance to right the biggest wrong she had ever committed.

"I guess we can't always get what we want," Bobbi whispered. The comment stung. Her older sister had wished death on her when she was the one recovering from giving birth to her twin's husband's illegitimate child.

Robbi wanted to say more, but the stiffness in her feet prevented her from speaking. She tried to wiggle her toes, but nothing moved, so she tried her feet and got the same response. Bobbi watched her eyes stare holes into her feet.

"Why did you do it?"

Robbi took her eyes from off her numb feet and redirected her attention to her sister.

"Because I wanted you to have your life back. It was a ploy to get you to leave him."

"And when it didn't work?"

"I fell for him."

Bobbi thought she'd have so much to say when she finally came face to face with Robbi. The last time she saw Robbi she had told her she was pregnant with Ruben's child. Bobbi never got the chance to express how she felt. Never got the chance to tell her that him getting her pregnant was only a way for him to control her, just like her having work done on her face was his way of controlling her. But now that she was back in front of Robbi, she had nothing to say.

"Walk away, Bobbi, and let it go."

Bobbi leaned her upper body forward, her hands folded and elbows planted on her thighs.

"I'll walk away when I make you go away," she whispered.

Robbi's eyes got big and then against her will, they slowly dropped. She felt her body become relaxed. Her eyes flew open and she opened her mouth to speak but nothing came out, her body rocking back and forth before finally falling back on the bed and becoming unconscious. Bobbi walked to Robbi's bedside and pressed the call button for a nurse. Seconds later Nurse Teller walked in with a middle-aged nurse, and Smith, dressed in scrubs. Bobbi retreated into the bathroom and changed into her surgical scrubs. When she reentered the room, the surgical instruments were neatly arranged, and everyone was stationed and ready to go.

Bobbi stood beside Smith, scared to actually partake in her dream.

"You make the first cut." Smith handed her the scalpel, his eyes never leaving Robbi.

Bobbi grabbed the instrument from Smith and he stepped out of her way. Bobbi cut into Robbi's face, doing exactly as Harvey had taught her.

"Cut into half of her face and let me do the rest." Smith was enraged, angry that his partner was dead, and he wanted revenge. He anticipated the moment Bobbi finished her part so that he could cut off Robbi's face and hold it in his hands.

Bobbi heard Smith but didn't comment. Instead, she concentrated on the barbaric act and didn't speak until she was finished. Nothing would ever be the same. In the short amount of time Bobbi and Harvey spent together, she could proudly admit that they were the greatest moments of her life; she thought she would live like that forever; she would have lived like that forever if it weren't for her husband. Now she had to take away everything he had, but before her journey of destruction could begin, she had to warn him and send him a gift.

Bobbi finished cutting, blood staining her gloves. She looked up at the nurses. The Russian woman observed the machinery while Nurse Teller dabbed the blood escaping Robbi's face so that the surgery wouldn't be difficult to carry out. Bobbi shook her head. *Why do we have all of this when we're going to kill her anyway?* she thought. But she didn't bother voicing that to Smith; he was the new Harvey once it came to the operating room, so she had to follow his lead.

Smith rushed over to Robbi. He cut into her face so swiftly and with such force, all three women jumped the second he made his first incision. He wasn't working with the mindset of a plastic surgeon, but with the emotion of a friend. Minutes later, Smith dropped the instrument on the tray and without bothering to use the proper equipment, with all his might, ripped her face off. He held it in his hands and laughed at his victory. The Russian nurse rushed to the bathroom and threw up her dinner, while Nurse Teller ignored the act and after taking the face from Smith, placed it in the proper packaging, then proceeded to clean up the room.

"When will she wake up?" Bobbi asked.

"She's not."

Bobbi looked at Smith, unaware of what he was talking about.

"You knocked her out and paralyzed her entire body. What are you talking about, she's not going to wake up?"

"She's dead, surprise!" Smith yelled, a smile plastered on his face.

Bobbi was surprised; she had no clue during her sister's facial removal that she was dead. They'd had an agreement that they would drug her, take off her face, and then kill her. Bobbi didn't know how to feel. Half of her was happy that her sister was gone and the other half angry that she wasn't the one to inject her with the deadly poison.

Her silence made Smith understand what he'd done. He took away what was meant for her to do.

"I'm sorry, I couldn't help myself. I guess I got carried away. It was too great of an opportunity to pass up. If hurting Ruben meant killing her, then I had to…"

Bobbi threw her hand in the air, cutting him off. "What did you just say?"

"I said it was too great of an..."

"No, before that."

Smith shut up, replaying his statement in his head. "I said I couldn't help myself. I guess I got carried away."

And just like that Bobbi was thrown into a time machine and taken back to the days when Harvey was alive.

"Harvey, keep fucking with my product and I'm going to send you to Colombia and have them stuff your balls with that shit."

"I'm sorry, sometimes I get a little carried away, and I can't help myself. Maybe if you let me play with yours sometimes, Bobbi, we wouldn't have this problem."

Bobbi ripped off her scrubs and gloves.

Bobbi snapped. "Deliver that shit with a bow and don't let it happen again." She raced into the bathroom, disregarding that the nurse was still in there throwing up. She grabbed her sunglasses from out of her purse and slapped them on her face. She was happy she'd worn clothing under her scrubs like Harvey had taught her so that she could race out of the room. The memories were suffocating, and she chose to run away from them. Her eyes watered under the shades. She wanted to get home and didn't want to communicate with anyone until she got the news that Ruben received her sister's face, the symbol of war.

Opening the door, Bobbi was confident that when she stepped foot out of the hospital, the doctors and nurses under her payroll would never admit to seeing her. She shut the door behind her and made a sharp right, bumping straight into Levi.

"What do you want to know first?" Levi asked.

5

"Tabitha runs the streets of Compton and oversees Ruben's corner boys. She's a loose cannon and wants nothing more than to take your place. Being on the frontline isn't doing it for her anymore and she's ready for a promotion. Ready to stand beside, Ruben."

"So she knows about me."

"Everyone knows about you; that's why she hates you. She's known in Compton, but you're known all over."

"Is she sleeping with him?"

"Yes"

"Other than the disrespect, is taking her out worth the hassle? I want to hurt his pockets, fuck his heart. I broke that shit when I kidnapped that little bastard and sold her to that couple."

"Killing off his Compton team won't break him, but it will hurt. If you're going to step foot there, you better take Tabitha out. If not, she will come for you. She's his muscle."

"His muscle? A female?"

"You run the East Coast, so why are you so surprised?"

Silence.

"Fine, bring her here to me. But don't let Ruben find out."

"Bring her here? How am I supposed to do that?"

"Sell her on her dream of knocking me off my pedestal, and when she's here, you'll be in L.A., knocking off her men, one by one."

That conversation felt like it took place years ago, but the truth of the matter was it only happened two weeks ago. Bobbi stood in her observation room with her hands behind her back, staring into the empty room. It was odd not seeing any work being done, but in this case, she needed privacy. Bobbi was expecting a visitor and she intended on giving Tabitha her full attention. She looked at the clock and the words *five more minutes* ran through her mind. Exactly five minutes later the bell rang, and Bobbi turned on the lobby's camera and saw Tabitha with three men by her side.

"That's not how you do business," Bobbi uttered to herself. She pushed the intercom and welcomed her. "You come up, but your men must stay."

"My men come with me," Tabitha responded.

"Then you all leave together. Thank you for coming."

Bobbi took her finger off the intercom button and waited for Tabitha's reaction. It was a game of divide and conquer, so she watched them divide.

For a moment Tabitha didn't move, she stood there thinking over the tight spot she was placed in. Although she knew five different ways to kill a human being with her bare hands, she didn't feel comfortable meeting Bobbi without her men. But greed got in the way, and the thought of taking her spot, overruled her gut feeling. Tabitha nodded toward the men and Bobbi watched them exit the building and stand outside. The bell rang again.

"I'm ready."

Bobbi buzzed Tabitha in and took one more look inside the neatly organized operating room. The two surgeons Harvey and Smith had trained, had earned their keep, and now worked as well as them. Bobbi looked up at the cameras over her head in time to see Tabitha exiting the elevator and heading her way. The main door had been left open so within ten seconds, Bobbi expected to see her at the waiting room. One by one, she turned off the five cameras, the last one showing Bobbi's men wean Tabitha's goons away from her building and ultimately out of their lives. Bobbi smiled. *Divide and conquer.*

Bobbi shut the screen off and turned away to see Tabitha standing at the door, looking at her through the plastic window. With her hand she signaled for her to turn the knob. With every step she took, Tabitha was falling deeper into Bobbi's trap.

Bobbi closed the curtains before Tabitha got a chance to look inside the surgery room that wasn't for her eyes to see yet.

"Tabitha, it's nice to finally meet you." Bobbi gave her a fake smile. Her huge, dark sunglasses concealed her real intentions.

"I was beginning to think you didn't know anything about me."

Bobbi walked over to her couch and took a seat. Before she responded, she looked her enemy over. The sides of Tabitha's head were shaven clean and the middle was slicked back into a high bun. She wore large gold-hoop earrings. Bobbi's eyes zeroed in on the tattoo printed on her collarbone: Ruben's name in plain sight.

"You're part of my business, therefore I know about you."

"Correction, I'm a part of *Ruben's* business."

"If that's what you want to believe."

"That's what I know."

Tabitha took it upon herself to sit directly across from Bobbi. Her legs opened and her folded hands dropped between them.

"I like you." Bobbi poured herself a small amount of vodka from the decanter in the middle of the table, and pretended to drink some, the liquid never going past her lips. "You remind me of myself."

Tabitha cringed at the statement.

"But like I said, I know everyone who works for me and that is why I want to offer you a promotion."

Tabitha noticed Bobbi didn't offer her a drink so she helped herself. She snatched the vodka and glass from off the table and poured a drink, emptying the decanter. She didn't care if there was nothing to mix the liquor with; she wanted to take the rest and leave Bobbi with nothing. Tabitha made Bobbi wait on her response while she drank her beverage, ignoring the salty taste.

Bobbi observed her consume the liquid without a care in the world.

"Good?" Bobbi asked.

Tabitha placed the glass down. "Terrific." A wide smile covered her face.

"Like I was saying," Bobbi's eyes looked at the clock, then back at Tabitha, "I want you to relocate to the East Coast and take over. It's lonely being a married woman in the big city while your husband is so far from you. I am ready to be in his presence and leave the Big Apple alone."

Bobbi gauged Tabitha's reaction. She watched as her breathing increased with every second that passed, while she replayed Bobbi's words. Tabitha's gut told her she should have told Ruben about her meeting. When Levi texted her that he put in a good word for her because Bobbi needed someone to take over the East Coast, she knew her dreams were coming true. But the second she was about to ask Ruben why he didn't bring this up to her himself, another text came in telling her not to mention it to Ruben. If he found out Bobbi was retiring, he'd try to talk her out of it. Tabitha was left weighing her options and wondering what meant more: telling Ruben what she was about to do even though he was against it, or keeping quiet and doing what she always wanted to do, gain more power and ultimately be his wife. Being his muscle was no longer what she wanted; her goals had changed and after being in the business for so many years, she now saw the bigger picture.

When Tabitha was first introduced to Levi, she smelled something fishy, but off the strength of Ruben, she let it go and wrote it off as her being overprotective about who entered their circle. But after getting that text, she was happy she stood down. He did nothing to ring any alarms the time he spent learning about Ruben's associates and business and 'til this day, there was still nothing shown for her to think that he couldn't be trusted.

"I have no disputes about taking your place." Tabitha smiled, ecstatic with the imagery. "But I don't think Ruben would be okay with this; what are his thoughts?" she asked, playing dumb.

"He does not like the idea of having both his women changing their positions."

Tabitha double blinked, the words *both his women*, catching her off-guard. Now it was Bobbi's turn to smile.

"But I will take care of my husband; all I need to hear from you is a yes or no, so what will it be?"

Bobbi waited for an answer that seemed to have a delayed response. Tabitha sat still on her couch, her eyes lowering, then flying back open. When it registered that she couldn't keep her eyes open, she slammed them shut, then opened them wide. She looked at Bobbi sitting in front of her, her figure sprinting into one big blur. Sweat formed on the sides of her head and with everything she had, she fought to reach for Bobbi's untouched drink. The room was spinning and a heat wave took over her. She devoured the drink, her mouth remaining open but no words stumbling out. She wrestled to breathe, but the uncomfortable feeling didn't last for long before calmness washed over her just in time for her body to collapse on the arm of the chair. When her body hit the chair, she slid off its leather and pounded against the floor, blacking out the second she came face to face with the floor tile.

"Watching you kill yourself makes me thirsty."

Bobbi recovered a bottle of water from the room's mini refrigerator, and after four gulps, finished the entire bottle. Hydrated and energized, she grabbed Tabitha by both hands and dragged her into the operating room.

"A war's going to break out. His baby mama's face was sent to him wrapped in plastic. I don't know if he lost his mind because that shit was disgusting, or because she was his girl."

Levi nodded, taking in everything he already knew from one of Ruben's workers who was having a drink. The men sat in the far back of a warehouse surrounded by each one of Ruben's employees who resided on the west side. The news of Robbi's death had spread like flames and left Ruben a destroyed man. He called a meeting in order to instruct everyone on their next move and called Levi back to L.A. Levi couldn't have been any more happier. Flying him back made his job ten times easier, and caused him to no longer wrack his brain as to how he would take care of Tabitha's men. Sitting in the warehouse, Levi was not only surrounded by Tabitha's crew, but Ruben's whole organization. This was the perfect opportunity to put a cap on his cousin's entire business.

Ruben walked in the room and when he stood in front of the crowd of people, his eyes found Levi and he signaled for him to come to the front. Levi finished his drink, put it on a table and headed toward his destination. The closer he got to Ruben, the more he witnessed the effects Robbi's death had on him. Ruben's eyes were red, skin clammy and clothing disheveled. He couldn't figure out for the life of him who was behind this crime and it was eating him alive.

"Did you hear anything over on the East Coast?" Ruben's back was turned toward the crowd and his voice low.

"No, you can hear a pen drop over there. What about here?"

"Nothing, but for some reason, I believe there's no one here that knows anything."

Levi's face scrunched up.

"Something tells me the answer is in New York." Ruben repeatedly nodded his head, stressing his belief.

"Why do you think that?"

"It's the only thing that makes sense; my weakest location is where I am not."

"Then why Robbi and not Bobbi?"

"I don't know, I don't know," Ruben constantly repeated. "But I know someone over there is responsible."

For a few days, Ruben held on to hope. He hoped that Robbi was still alive after receiving her face, but that wish was shattered when the search party he sent out to her couldn't locate her. The hospital had no records of her or his daughter, and the world was trying to make him believe they didn't exist. The stress of it all was driving him mad.

"You're reaching Ruben."

Ruben ignored his cousin and filled him in on what would happen next. "They're all going back to New York with you, and you're going to ensure they find her killer."

Before Levi could respond, Ruben turned toward the group of men and proceeded to speak. Standing behind his cousin, all Levi could do was smile. Ruben was determined to get revenge, but Levi was the only person in the room who knew that would never happen.

"My woman's killer is not close by; they're in New York. And if they're in New York, then that's where we need to be."

No one spoke, instead they all allowed their thoughts to race through their mind, waiting until one guess was crowned correct.

"You all are going there and you're not coming back until you find out who is responsible. I don't care if you have to fuckin' rip the worm out of the Big Apple. Find her killer. And the first person who does will become my partner." Business was no longer a priority for Ruben. He didn't care if he left the West Coast empty without activity, he wanted Robbi's murderer found.

A sea of smiles invaded the room. Ruben was a greedy, cheap man who controlled with fear and made everyone scared to go against him, but if they became his partner, they no longer had to worry about light pockets. Ruben spoke a little more and when he finished, whispered for Levi to take the floor; he would be in charge while in New York.

"Whatever you have to say, say it now," Ruben whispered. "I have a few things to take care of before you all leave."

Before Levi had a chance to say a word, Ruben left the building, unknowingly leaving his men to die.

For a total of five minutes, Levi fed the group of men a bunch of bull, then left them to talk amongst themselves. He quickly slid out the room and locked up the last exit to the building once outside. Levi jumped inside his car and drove around the corner to a secluded neighborhood. Sitting in the dark, he texted one of Bobbi's workers, *Do it.* Ten seconds later, a loud explosion was heard and car alarms went off. The text message, *it's done*, was sent directly to Bobbi's phone.

6

One hour later

Covered in darkness, Ruben reflected back on his life. The image of Robbi's decaying face sitting in plastic was frozen in his mind and encircled with the question of *who did this?* The heavy breathing from the naked, sleeping woman helped him maintain his sanity. He listened to her lungs suck air in and out with every breath she took. He focused more on not breaking down. While taking a temporary vacation to the past, Ruben's phone lit up and the sound of a cash register rang throughout the room, alerting him of a text message.

What time is the meeting?

Ruben smirked while shaking his head. Lawson was the irresponsible screw-up in his crew. He would have been gone a long time ago if it wasn't for his killer instincts and ties with Tabitha. In this business, Lawson was Tabitha's shadow and right hand. She was her brother's keeper and did everything she could to keep him employed, including degrading herself for Ruben's sick needs.

Ruben's fingers pounded down against the phone's buttons. It wasn't until then did he notice Lawson wasn't present at the meeting. In the middle of the text, he stopped, his mind drifting off to the group of men stationed in the warehouse. *Where was Tabitha? Why wasn't she at the meeting?* Ruben shot him the text, his leg shaking in anticipation of his response.

Tabitha's in New York, you didn't know?

Ruben's eyes grew and without giving it a second thought proceeded to respond, but before he got the chance to hit the *send* button, Lawson sent another text.

Your wife sent for her not too long after your girl's death. How didn't you know? Let me find out you can't keep up with all them females? Lol.

Immobile, Ruben stared into space. He had thought of everyone he figured had a reason to kill Robbi. Everyone except for Bobbi. And now that he'd seen the truth, he understood why she would want to hurt him and go as far as to murder her own blood. Bobbi had all the tools needed to carry out this mission and more than enough motivation. Ruben's free hand balled into a fist.

Why didn't you go with her? he typed.

Minutes later Lawson responded. *She told me not to. She wanted me to stay behind and watch over your business.*

Back to back Bobbi snapped pictures with her Polaroid camera. Like a running faucet photographs leaked from out the camera and splashed onto the surgical room's floor. A river of photos led from her feet to the middle of the room. Bobbi took her final shot, then lowered the camera from her face to admire her work. Tabitha's boob job had Harvey written all over it. She took her time when performing the surgery and allowed his voice to guide her hands. She missed him terribly. The more she practiced her craft, the more it validated that if Harvey were alive, she would have been his protégé.

Bobbi placed the white sheet over Tabitha's body, tucking her into bed one last time. The GHB worked better than she had expected. When she started the surgery, the drug sent Tabitha into a coma, then fifteen minutes into the operation, killed her. The machines rang throughout the room, but Bobbi ignored them, continuing to insert the implants. "Moonlight Sonata" occupied the room, and memories of the month's past events, drove her to tears. Tears filled the surgical mask. Life was hard, but living it alone was harder. The tranquility and constant replay of "Moonlight Sonata" whenever the CD player tried to move to the next song, informed Bobbi of Harvey's presence. While operating in the past, Harvey never liked listening to anything other than that song. His tyranny over the music selection started many disputes between him and Smith, and left Bobbi with multiple headaches. But now that she stood there alone while operating on a corpse, she wished their bickering would return.

Bobbi touched the scar Harvey removed from her chest. She thought about the surgeries he never got the chance to perform on her face.

Finally, the music stopped. Bobbi stared down at the covered corpse. The sight of Tabitha's body told the story of how this situation came to be and made her question how Ruben found out about her infidelity. *He probably had eyes on me*, she thought. Drained, Bobbi gazed at the ceiling, her heart yearning for Harvey. Seconds later she walked inside the observation room where she removed her scrubs and plopped down on the couch, a need to reenergize illustrated on her face. Thoughts of Harvey filled her mind but quickly dwindled when the continuous ringing of her cell ripped her out of her place of solitude. Irritated, she dug inside her purse with the goal of turning it off, but when her cell phone touched the palm of her hand, it stopped ringing and a text message came through.

You bitch. I made you and now I'm going to kill you.

Bobbi smiled. After receiving his gift, some way, somehow, Ruben had solved the puzzle as to whom had killed Robbi. *Now this is going to be fun*, she thought.

You created a monster. Now watch me terrorize you. Keep your eye out for the mailman because your next delivery is on its way, she texted.

There were two things in life Ruben loved most: women and money. So Bobbi was going to give him what he wanted—Tabitha stuffed with heroin-filled implants.

She exited out of Ruben's text message and saw Levi's notification that the job was done. *Get out of LA now*, was all she wrote back.

7

"Ruben didn't tell you his connects' current contact information, but I have everything that you need. So move fast and cut off his supply. He had his suspicions about Robbi's killer being in New York, but after being tipped off about Tabitha meeting up with you, he now knows you're behind Robbi's murder."

"Who told him Tabitha was here?"

"Her brother. The only person who wasn't in the warehouse when it burned down. Ruben put two and two together after speaking with Lawson."

"Did he receive Tabitha?"

"Yes. Her and the double D's filled with heroin. That's another reason why you have to move fast. You're hitting him nonstop and making it impossible for him to fight back. He's not going to be your punching bag for much longer. He told me to kill you, and to make sure it's done, he'll be flying Tabitha's brother out here."

"Even after the warehouse burned down, he still hasn't connected you to any of this?"

"No, so contact his connect now because Lawson is on his way."

It was the day after Ruben had contacted Bobbi, and her discussion with Levi that morning was fresh in her mind. Bobbi didn't know everything about her husband, but she did know he wouldn't strike right away; he wanted her to live in fear and like a child, avoid every dark corner with thoughts of him being there. Ruben was addicted to control and once he had a hold of her mind, he planned to strike when she least expected it. However, her familiarity with his obsession to dominate her put her ten steps ahead and gave her more time to torture him. While he sat playing mind games, she kept throwing jabs and watching his world crumble. Going for the final blow, Bobbi dialed Priscilla. Three rings later, her Colombian voice came alive on the line.

"Long time no speak," Priscilla sang into the phone.

"Hello, Cilla, how are you?"

"I am well."

Priscilla was the wife of Ruben's connect, Jorge. She lived inside a world where they trusted no one and was locked inside a bubble her husband claimed was for her own protection. The hold Ruben had on Bobbi made Jorge comfortable with the two women forming a friendship. Priscilla didn't have a lot of friends, so meeting someone who understood her lifestyle was a breath of fresh air. The couple had no idea Bobbi didn't receive their new contact information. It was all a part of Ruben's plan to keep Bobbi beneath him.

"Tell me, old friend, what are your plans for tomorrow?"

Priscilla inhaled, then released her breath, frustrated that every day she had the same answer. "Nothing, but at least I won't be home alone. The exterminator will be here in the morning." This was her way of telling Bobbi that Jorge would be home.

"You're right; you won't be home alone because I'll be visiting."

"You lie!" Priscilla screamed, excitement punched in every word. Having a chance to entertain someone other than Jorge's business associates was a great distraction and made it possible for her to live a life outside of his.

"Nope, I speak the truth. If you'll have me, I'll be there tomorrow."

"Of course you're welcome! But give me one second to check on my fish."

Bobbi remained quiet, accepting that Priscilla had to go check with Jorge. Normal tell-all conversations didn't happen during their phone calls; they lived a life where everything was irregular. Priscilla muted the phone and returned in less than a minute.

"Sorry about that, I had to check my food. I can't have it burning, but like I said you are more than welcomed. Now let me go, I have a lot of work to do." In Priscilla's world this meant she had to start preparing a large spread, put fresh flowers in her guest room and make a list of everything she wanted to speak about.

"I will see you soon." Bobbi hung up her cell phone, her carry-on bag positioned beside her and ready for departure.

From the second Bobbi touched down on Colombian soil, she had either been running around or at a table eating. Priscilla ran her ragged while out on the town and constantly stuffed food down her throat in order for her to experience Colombia in its entirety. Bobbi was five pounds heavier and exhausted by the time they made it back to Priscilla's home. It had been years since Bobbi last had a girl's day out, especially one without people glaring at her face. All of Colombia knew who Priscilla was, so while she enjoyed the day with Bobbi, everyone kept their eyes straight and acted as if the women didn't exist.

"Bobbi, why are you here? Why visit?" Priscilla asked, her eyes taking in the sights of the city from inside the car. She didn't know when she'd be able to venture out again.

"I'm here to see you."

"No you don't. You come a little to see me. What business do you have with Jorge?" After asking the question, Priscilla looked at Bobbi with sadness spread across her face. The defeated look reminded Bobbi that although she walked around with a damaged outer shell, there was one thing she had that Priscilla wished upon a star for—freedom. Priscilla was a prisoner within her own life. Nothing in her world was one hundred percent hers. She shared it all with Jorge.

Bobbi sat quiet for a minute. She didn't mean to use Priscilla in order to get to her husband, but it was the way of their world, and friendship couldn't come in the way.

"You know I can't tell you that, Priscilla."

Priscilla shook her head and looked up; she lived her life for a man she could only know bits and pieces about. "You used me to get here, so now that you're here, you tell me."

Hearing her speak brought Bobbi back to when they first met. Back then Priscilla knew very little English but listening to her now, Bobbi could see that she had come a long way. Jorge spoke English fluently and therefore, his wife sought to learn the language. Priscilla wouldn't look Bobbi's way while waiting for an answer she knew she wasn't allowed to hear, but she had to know. For once she had to be more than just a trophy wife. Bobbi looked out the window; her friend was fighting for an identity, dying to be someone other than her husband's wife. Telling her this little bit of information would give something to Priscilla she needed, a purpose.

"This is between us," Bobbi informed her.

Priscilla nodded her head.

"Ruben will no longer do business with Jorge because I will be taking his place."

"The only way Jorge will do business with you is if Ruben dies or betrays him. That I do know. That much he does tell me."

"I know."

Question marks were stamped all over Priscilla's face when she looked Bobbi's way. "What are you saying, he's dead or he betrayed Jorge?" Concerned, her eyes begged for Bobbi not to tell her a war was about to break out due to disloyalty.

"I'm saying that Jorge will *believe* Ruben has deceived him, and as for him being dead, that will transpire in due time." Bobbi looked closely into Priscilla's eyes. She asked for the truth and now that it was given to her, she had to swallow it whole. She told her flat out that she was going to lie on her husband and slide into his seat.

"Why? Why lie? You have freedom; isn't that enough?"

"You have beauty and love; isn't that enough?"

Silence stumped into the car like a bulldozer ramming into rubble. Priscilla had heard the rumors about Ruben forcing Bobbi to get plastic surgery and about her having an affair, but she and Jorge didn't believe it nor did they pay it any mind. When it came to Jorge's associates' private life, he turned a deaf ear.

"I won't tell. But promise me when it's done, you'll come back to visit me."

"I'll do you one better. I'll send for you. That way, I'll get the chance to run you ragged and make you fat."

The women laughed, both proud they had a friend who understood them outside of their husbands.

8

After Bobbi's departure, Priscilla couldn't help but wonder if she'd gotten away with the tale she'd told and if so, did Jorge live up to his word and agree to work with her. The suspense was killing Priscilla. She planned to ask Bobbi the outcome, but she had left immediately after speaking with Jorge. Piecing together what she imagined their conversation consisted of, Jorge walked into their bedroom and removed his robe. The sight of him caused Priscilla to shake with every move he made. A piece of her scolded her to shut up, stay in her place, while another part urged her to open her mouth, and dare to ask a question. Jorge slid into bed and grabbed his wife's hand.

"You liked having your friend here, didn't you?"

"Yes."

"Good because you will be seeing more of her."

"Is that so?"

For a brief moment Jorge remained quiet as if searching for the proper words.

"For a woman to set out to destroy her husband, proves the heart is stronger than any control a husband has over his wife. He broke her and I don't want that to be you, so I am going to work with her. Use her heartache to make me money and examine her ways so that I will know what not to do to you."

Priscilla was speechless. All it took was for one life to end in order for hers to begin. Holding back tears, Priscilla pushed herself to ask, "How do you know it is her intentions to destroy him?"

"Because Ruben is a dirty man, and although I never took notice into his personal life, I knew the rumors were true. But for your sake, I pretended they weren't. You have enough things to worry about. The last thing I need to do is add to your list of thoughts whether or not I will break your spirit."

Tears dropped from Priscilla's cheeks. The honesty was astonishing. "What now? What will happen to Ruben?"

"I'll take care of him, sort of like my welcome-to-the-family gift for Bobbi."

Priscilla turned on her side, facing her husband with wide eyes. "She doesn't know what you're going to do?"

"No and keep it to yourself; things like this is what will keep her loyal."

9

"Why the fuck didn't you kill her three days ago when you were supposed to?"

"The timing was never right, but after being the one to find Tabitha's body in front of Ruben's house, aren't you happy I dropped the ball?"

Silence.

"She'll be flying in tonight. Act as her driver and get her then. She's never seen you before, Lawson, so there's no reason anything should go wrong. She'll be the only female on that jet, and all of the things you heard about her face is true, so don't stare. That's the only thing that will fuck you up from getting close to her. She doesn't speak much and more than likely she'll be wearing dark shades, as a way of concealing her face, and combat boots. Her hair is also wild. It covers the majority of her face."

"Notes taken. What time will she be landing?"

"At eleven p.m. Don't be late."

Lawson was late for everything in his life, but tonight he was two hours early waiting on Bobbi to land. The conversation between Levi and him replayed in his mind a number of times; he wanted to make sure he got the right woman. He'd heard about Bobbi, but never had he seen her in person. Inside his lap sat a sketch of what he envisioned Bobbi to look like. He planned to get one good look at her without staring and compare it to his drawing. Maybe after avenging his sister's death, he'd try his hand at becoming an artist.

Twenty minutes later, Lawson looked inside his side-view mirror and saw a head of big hair, and a woman draped in black, walking his way. He looked at his drawing one last time, then jumped out of the limo. The closer she got to the car, the more of Levi's description was checked off his list. The last thing he noticed were her heavy leather boots. She approached the car and he opened the door, her eyes fixated on his face.

"Who are you? And where's Lehman?"

Levi never warned him that she may speak, but he was quick on his feet when responding.

"I'm Stone. I don't know what happened to Lehman, but I got a call from Levi directing me to come and pick you up so I didn't ask any questions."

Bobbi nodded her head. "Good."

Bobbi got into the limo and seconds later, Lawson was back in the driver's seat. The partition window was completely down when Bobbi positioned herself directly in front of it and Lawson hoped she wouldn't roll it up. Her sitting there made his job ten times easier. Minutes later, while on the road, the divider remained in place and Lawson was content with putting his plan into action. He made a left where he should have made a right and drove onto a road surrounded by trees. The more he drove, the deeper into the forest they got.

"Pull over, I have to piss."

Bobbi's vulgar language showed that she was anything but a lady, and because of that, Lawson now understood why she thought she could get away with killing Tabitha. She thought she was one of the boys.

Lawson smirked. "Sure."

This wasn't how he'd planned to kill her, but why not; she was making her death extremely easy and inevitable. He drove off the road and deeper into the darkness. Lawson put the car in *park* and after his fingers grabbed a hold of his gun beneath his seat, bullets entered his skull and blew his head off. Brain fragments littered the car's interior and plastered Bobbi's face like a bad prosthetic makeup job.

"Shit. I always forget that shit happens." She grabbed a shirt from out of her carry-on bag and cleaned herself off. Quickly, she changed into a new outfit and waited for Levi to pull up beside her. Lawson's work ethic was so sloppy he never noticed Levi and another one of her men following a distance behind them. The three switched cars and Bobbi drove off, leaving the men to take care of the mess.

10

Exiting off the dirt road, Bobbi thought of her sins. After everything she'd done to ruin Ruben's life, she was sure she would have had more leeway to breathe. But the closer she got to destroying him for good, the more disconnected and uncomfortable she felt with life. The lack of air transporting through her lungs forced her foot to crash down harder on the gas. With her mouth agape, she inhaled deeply. Tears surged to the brim of her eyes. Without warning, she released a howling, glass-scratching scream. However, nothing she was doing was easing the pain, let alone filling the void. All she wanted was Harvey, and no matter how much Ruben suffered, it didn't trump her need to be loved. It wasn't until that moment did she realize the more she did to Ruben, the more unfulfilled she felt.

Taking off at the speed of light, Bobbi never stood a chance of slamming down on the brakes before hitting the man staggering across the road. So with only a second to make a drastic decision, she made a sharp left turn, the wheels squeaking in the wind. Tire marks stained the ground and glistened under the midnight after the automobile flipped over and slid across the road, coming to a halt seconds later. Three men, including the staggering stranger, stepped out from the darkness and ran to the car in minutes before it blew up. They pulled Bobbi from the demolished vehicle and threw her into a Jeep pulling up to the scene.

Bobbi's eyes repeatedly opened and closed when her body touched the Jeep's leather interior. The gash on her forehead and busted chin spewed blood. The Jeep drove off and when Bobbi was able to keep her eyes open for more than two seconds, her vision focused in on Ruben. Her head was in his lap.

"I got to give it to you; I would have never thought you'd turn my own cousin against me. But I guess anything is possible. And who knew following my fuck-up of a worker, Lawson, would have led me to all of this. You're slipping, Bobbi. Next time, pay attention to who's following your backup. But I got to hand it to you; you got them all, Bobbi. You got them all good."

And that was the last thing Bobbi heard before temporarily blacking out.

11

After an hour of being beaten in the face with brass knuckles, Bobbi became numb to any other hit given to her. Seconds before blacking out, she caught a glimpse of the crystal clock she'd picked out for Ruben's home, hanging on the living room wall.

He brought me back to L.A.? He's going to kill me on his territory.

Her eyes closed just in time before Ruben could land another blow, but this time they didn't reopen because they had swollen shut. Her vision was taken, leaving Bobbi with nothing but her hearing.

"You think I fucked up your face before; wait until you see what I did now!"

Ruben dropped down beside Bobbi sprawled out on the carpet and grabbed a handful of her hair, forcing her to lift her head up. In his free hand, he held a mirror up to her face.

"Look!" he demanded, but Bobbi's eyelids never opened. The heaviness prevented her from showing her irises. "I said look!" He pulled back Bobbi's head harder, her hair ripping from its roots. Frantic, Ruben pushed her right eyelid up until her entire eyeball was visible. "Look! Don't you look great?"

Bobbi could barely see. Everything was blurry and glimpses of shadows flashed before her eyes. But with enough willpower she looked back at the person staring at her from the mirror. She used to think she was unrecognizable before, but she was wrong. There was no trace of her old face left. Her nose was crooked and bottom lip busted open so deep, it was split in two, the bottom half dangling from a piece of flesh. With what little energy she had left she tried shaking her hair from out of Ruben's grasp. Her sudden movements caught him off-guard and she rammed her head into his chin, his mouth crashing shut and a tooth escaping. Ruben let go of Bobbi and fell backward. Landing on his back, he screamed out in pain while rolling around and clutching his mouth, blood seeping between his fingers.

Short of breath, Bobbi crawled to the other side of the room where the mirror was thrown. After feeling around for it and finally discovering its location, she slammed her fist down on the glass, shattering it. She grabbed the biggest piece she thought she felt. Terrified and seemingly blind, she felt around for something sturdy. She pulled herself up onto her feet, using a bookcase shelf.

Finding her balance, Ruben raced toward her and slammed her body against a row of books. The impact knocked the wind out of her and sent her crashing to the floor. She fought to breathe and then it hit her: if she didn't fight harder, she was going to die. With the glass in hand and Ruben hovering over her, she prayed when she tried to stab him that she'd succeed. She cocked her hand back and with all her might caught him in the leg. Automatically, Ruben's body slithered down the books and collapsed on top of Bobbi, blood seeping through his clothes and making its way through hers.

She wiggled out from underneath him and after still having difficulty seeing, she took her fingers and forced her eyes open. When she did she saw a group of Colombian men with silencers on their guns, pointing her way.

12

Four months later

It took a number of surgeries to get Bobbi's face to look one pinch decent. Smith tried talking her into letting him do more. He was sure that later on, he could fix her appearance and make her look normal again, but Bobbi declined. If it wasn't for the severity of her new facial wounds, she wouldn't have even agreed to him touching her face to begin with. She needed the surgery but the *extra* work Smith wanted to do was more along the lines of cosmetic and not a necessity. She wasn't willing to let anyone who wasn't Harvey touch her face for cosmetic reasons.

Everything that remotely reminded her of Ruben was removed. His crew, home, women and the way he conducted business. Everything except for Jorge had been changed and revamped to what Bobbi wanted. After Jorge's hit men took her to safety and got her medical attention, he informed her of his part in Ruben's murder. Bobbi wanted to be angry for not killing Ruben herself, but she had to give props when they were due, and be happy Jorge intervened when he had, because if he hadn't, she may not have lived.

That afternoon Bobbi temporarily traded in her Yankees fitted for a huge, black floppy hat. Sitting upright in her lounge chair beside her pool, she sat comfortably while reading a novel. After finishing chapter fourteen, she picked her eyes up and saw Levi heading her way. She read the first three sentences of chapter fifteen and waited for Levi to disrupt her reading. But when he sat down and didn't speak, she continued reading.

Bobbi drank some of her juice, then grabbed the pitcher of lemonade and poured him a nice tall glass of his own. She pushed the drink toward him and went back to her reading.

Levi had called her up that morning telling her that he would like to meet with her. It was ninety-five degrees, a perfect day for a drink by the pool so Bobbi invited him over. Levi inhaled the sweet drink, devouring it within a few seconds.

"I needed that, can I have more?" Levi nodded toward the pitcher. And without her looking his way, Bobbi moved her head up and down. After another glass and a half, the pitcher was more than halfway empty. Levi looked at the glass and finally spoke.

"You wanna hear something funny. That night you took Lawson out and Ruben's men rolled up on me, the first thing that flashed before my eyes were Buffalo wings and lemonade. I was like, damn, these motherfuckers are gonna kill me and I'll never have Buffalo wings or lemonade again." Levi laughed. "But I'm glad that gun dude had to my head, jammed. That one second gave me enough time to take them all out." Levi rewound back to that dreadful night and when he came back to the present, noticed Bobbi was lost in her world of reading and paying him no mind. So he cut to the chase.

"I wanted to thank you. I got a call from my brother a few weeks ago telling me you paid his debt off months ago. I don't know why he didn't tell me sooner, but then again, it doesn't matter, as long as it's paid off."

"About that...the debt isn't paid off." Bobbi turned the page, her reading glasses making the letters appear twice as clear.

"What are you talking about? My brother left me a..."

Cutting him off, Bobbi finished his sentence. "Message saying that I paid the debt off and he is now away on vacation. He's sorry for leaving without you knowing, but after being in hiding for so long, he needed to get away."

"How did you know that?"

Bobbi removed her glasses, grabbed her bookmark from off the small table, and placed it between chapter fifteen's second and third pages.

"Because I told him to say it, and when he refused, I told him I'd kill you if he didn't." Bobbi's lifeless stare told him everything he needed to know.

"You set me up."

"You see, Levi, Ruben was the one who put the hit out on Harvey, but you carried it out. Did you really think everyone would get what they deserved, but *you?*"

"What did you do to my brother?" Sweat dropped from Levi's face and he found himself battling to breathe. "What did you do to my brother!" he yelled. His change of behavior didn't startle her, so she drank the last of her juice before answering.

"I killed him. You really should have hid him better."

Frozen and fighting off a dizzy spell, Levi forced himself to speak. "You planned this all along. You found out everything about me after I killed your boyfriend, didn't you? You would have killed me right then and there if you didn't need information on Ruben first."

"Of course, anything else wouldn't make sense."

Levi's body became still, alerting him that his demise was only moments away. A short moment later, he toppled over, his face hitting the ground.

"I assume you don't like GHB in your drink. You should have had fruit punch like me." Bobbi took her book from off her lap and placed it on the table. Standing up, she grabbed his head and repeatedly bashed it against the ground until she was sure he was dead. When she felt for his pulse and no movements were discovered, she got back up, and with her foot, pushed him into the pool, his body splashing water from out its habitat and onto land.

Bobbi snatched the towel from off the arm of her chair and cleaned the blood coloring her skin. When that was complete, she sat back down, grabbed her book, and set out to finish chapter fifteen.

Born and raised in New York City, Brandie Davis graduated with a Bachelor's degree in English from York College and is the founder of My Urban Books blog and Facebook book club. In 2012 Brandie grabbed readers' attention with her debut novel, Renee: All Hail the Queen, *and the next year released its sequel,* Renee 2: The Protégé. *From home she continues to pen drama-filled novels. Contact the author: Twitter: @AuthorBrandieD; www.brandiedavisauthor.com; www.facebook.com/brandie.davis.948*

BY N'TYSE

1

"That's right. Suck this, big, python bitch! Ooooh shiiiit," Keyz groaned. "Do it like that...yeah, spit on it," he instructed. His head fell back against the butter-soft leather of the maroon-painted, old school Chevy Impala. His bloodshot eyes began to drift involuntarily to the back of his head, denying him of that pornographic presentation. It was like she was sucking the life out of him the way she swallowed his dick whole. He lifted his left hand and wrapped his fingers in all fourteen inches of the prostitute's platinum blonde weave, never breaking her rhythm. He pushed her head farther into his lap until his dick was throwing jabs at the back of her throat and his sweaty nuts were waxing her chin.

"You like that, daddy?" the woman managed in between her oral beatdown.

"Hoe, I said don't talk. Suck!" Keyz commanded while he pumped the hooker's mouth like an oil well. She bottled every inch of him and with the constant swerve of her warm tongue, Keyz could feel his orgasm rising to the occasion. "Oh shit!" he muttered repeatedly, making her work double overtime for her hundred-dollar fee. Keyz outstretched his right hand and grabbed a handful of her round, juicy derriere. He hiked up her dress, stole a peek of her black lace thong, and slid his middle finger down the crack of her ass. He determined instantly that he would fuck her before the night was over.

Keyz was high as a kite and the potent aroma of fresh weed still lingered in his clothing and on his breath. He was the type to stay blazed from sunup to sundown. Weed was his medicine. He was so addicted to that Kush that he would choose a high over a female any day of the week. But like any other medicine, there were side effects, and at that moment, Keyz was so horny and delusional that he thought his anorexic five-inch dick was going to somehow rip out the woman's tonsils and pop out of the back of her head.

As she made sweet love to him orally, Keyz imagined all the freaky things he would do to her later that night—after his drop. He had made plans in his mind to head back over to her post, scoop her up, and take her to his place so that she could get another taste of the python. Judging how desperate she seemed for money, he knew she would hop on the opportunity. Keyz never had a problem paying for sex. He had bank. What he got out of it the most was convenience. He preferred his women the way he preferred his meals—on the go and made-to-order. He was too busy stacking paper to be stuck on a broad. That's why his motto was "Fuck the bitch, pay the bitch, and toss her ass before sunrise." Never in his life had he ever been caught up.

His tongue began to tingle and trickles of sweat skated down both sides of his chubby face. His erection pulsated in excitement and his heart raced like a turbo engine from the work she was putting in. He still couldn't believe he was getting lip service from a woman this fine. The longer she showered and sucked on his head, the more his curiosity peaked. He couldn't wait to test out that pussy later tonight.

"Oooooh, this a real big nut coming for you, baby," he warned. He forced his eyes completely open, as weak and tight as they were from lack of sleep. He wanted to watch her finish him off. She flicked her long tongue across his swollen head. That alone should have been enough to make him bust his load, but he was holding on for as long as he possibly could. He wanted to get every bit of his money's worth. She looked up at him, unlocked her jaws, and shoved him right back down her throat.

Right at the brink of dumping his load into her mouth, his car shook violently, rocking him like a baby, and knocking the hooker into the dashboard.

"Owwww!" The woman rubbed the right side of her head.

"Got damn!" Keyz hollered. He practically pushed the prostitute away from him. He twisted his body to look behind them. "This motherfucker done hit my shit!" The only thing he was able to see through the limo tint on his car's windows were bright headlights. Vexed, he turned back around, huffing and puffing like he'd run a marathon. He was barely able to lift his large body off the seat to slide his boxers and jeans back up, let alone conceal his erection. A murderous rage ripped through him and he was ready to beat a cat's head wide open to a bloody pulp for ramming into his whip.

He hopped out of the car looking madder than a Bulldog. He yelled obscenities, but before approaching the midnight-black Cadillac Escalade that had rear-ended him, he stopped to survey the damage on his car. He became even more heated the second he saw that his bumper was dented and his paint severely scratched. The mug plastered on his face didn't come close to revealing how ham he was about to go on that no-driving son-of-a-bitch.

Without the five carats sparkling in his ears, Keyz's tar-black skin seemingly allowed him to camouflage in the darkness. In many instances, it worked to his advantage. To those that didn't know him personally, he looked like an ordinary overweight black man. However, the six teardrops underneath both his eyes, which were almost invisible to the human eye because of his dark pigmentation, weren't there for the hell of it. They were the stripes that he'd earned for getting his hands dirty. The rewards for putting in work. Those tattoo tears weren't simply cosmetic. They were his street credentials for the bodies he had caught carrying out hood justice.

"Ugghh!" he fumed. With his fists balled at his sides, Keyz stormed toward the SUV. "Muhfucka, you ain't see my shit parked right there?" he barked at the hooded individual slumped over the stirring wheel. He paused. "Say my nigga, is you deaf or something? You fucked up my ride, cuz." He was ready to knock this fool's block off.

At only five-six with a three-hundred-thirty-five-pound body frame of mostly fat and very little muscle, he intimidated the hardest of them all. He was notorious for beating heads to the white meat singlehandedly. He was a head-buster, bone crusher, and somebody that nobody wanted to have beef with.

When Keyz didn't receive a response, he took a single step forward. Merely inches away.

"Say, podna! You hear me talking to you?" he seethed. Keyz spoke a lot louder this time. He was so infuriated the steam coming out of his nose felt like tear gas. He looked around him. Before he could breathe another word or make a false move, the hooded figure rose up, and in one swift move, pressed the rose-pink nine-millimeter firmly underneath his chin. He flinched the instant that cold piece of metal osculated his Adam's apple.

Shinette dropped her hoodie, displaying long and bouncy jet-black curls that fell evenly over her shoulders. Her round, charcoal, beady eyes were reduced to slits.

"You say something, motherfucker?"

Keyz slowly raised his hands in defeat. He was certain he'd never seen her before, because *that* face, he would have definitely remembered. The entire left side of it was covered with a tribal snake tattoo. The king cobra had a 3-D effect and appeared to be coming out of her skin. While going for her throat was his first thought, he trusted his instincts that if she was as crazy as she looked, he'd be rotting by morning. It was a chance he didn't want to take. Not tonight. Not when he still had five kilos of cocaine in the back of his trunk to unload.

"Look, before this gets outta hand, why don't you go ahead and put—"

"You fat, black, cockeyed fuck, did we ask you to speak?" Tierra retorted, her .45 leveled at the back of Keyz's head.

He took slow, deep breaths, clenched his jaws, and bit down hard on his bottom lip. "I can't believe this shit," he muttered.

Reality finally settled in and he grasped the fact that he had been set up. The young and sexy amazon he had picked up tonight was incognito. She was only posing as a hooker to throw him off and her strategy had worked. As she lured him into a dark alley, it had never crossed Keyz's mind that the plan all along was to rob him. For the full fifteen minutes that Tierra had seduced him, she had caused him to lose sight of everything, including the trade he was due to make in a half hour. Now he was in a no-win situation. Two bitches, two guns, but only one Keyz.

"Feeling froggy, motherfucker?" Shinette smiled sinisterly as she stared him dead in the eyes, reading his every thought. She repositioned the gun and aimed right between his sockets.

"Man, just take what the fuck y'all want and be out."

Shinette's deceiving smile faded and that menacing glare returned.

Like a terrible yeast infection, her trigger finger itched to pull back and let go. She wanted to pop his ass so bad, her pussy started throbbing from the rush. She stroked the belly of the gun, adrenaline coursing through her veins.

"Better yet, how about y'all take the three hundred in my pocket, ride out, and I'll pretend that none of this shit ever happened," Keyz lied, hoping to strike a bargain. He knew that if nothing else was certain in this world, payback was. He never would have allowed them to get away with this. Plus, he had a photographic memory so they didn't stand a chance at making it out of Dallas alive. He was going to make sure they paid with not only their lives, but the lives of their loved ones. He almost felt sorry for them because it was apparent to Keyz that they obviously didn't know who they had set out to rob. He was convinced they were amateurs who would soon learn the hard way that they weren't about the life.

Shinette tossed Tierra the duct tape.

"Come on," Keyz bribed. "It ain't even gotta go down like this. If it's money you want, I can help you with that. These guns are unnecessary," he carried on, waiting for the right moment to strike.

Shinette didn't budge, only stared at him crazy, telepathically delivering confirmation that he had been their target. This wasn't a fly-by-night-stickup or an unplanned heist. Not by far. She was way too smart for that. He had failed to realize that one of the most cunning, ruthless, diabolical she-devils from the Greedy Grove had sought him out. Keyz was a transporter. That was why they had been tracking him for months, waiting for the right time to strike. His sweet tooth for trashy pussy turned out to work in their favor. But what really got him marked was that he was too sloppy and arrogant for his own good. Thought he couldn't be touched. Thought he had the triple D sewed up.

The explosion of fireworks sounded off and could be heard near and far—the perfect diversion for a clean getaway. As time ticked away, what seemed like a lifetime to Keyz had only been three minutes and fifty-one seconds. Tierra quickly unrolled the tape and cautiously reached for Keyz's left hand. Predicting his fate, Keyz grabbed the gun in front of him. Before Tierra could second-guess herself, she unloaded a single bullet into the back of his cranium.

Keyz took a couple of drunken steps backward before completely losing his balance and dropping to the pavement.

Tierra recoiled in shock from the sight of all the blood and brain matter that oozed from the back of Keyz's head. Her face and dress had been splattered as well, causing her to panic. She looked down at her feet and the forming puddle of blood Keyz lay in, trailed in her direction. She moved her feet before the blood could stain her shoes. Her heart pumped loudly through her chest and her stomach tightened in knots. The cold chrome metal seemed to melt in Tierra's sweaty palm once she realized what she had done. She couldn't maintain her grip, and before she knew it, the gun slipped out of her hands.

Shinette quickly hopped out of the stolen vehicle, pistol trained on Keyz's squirming body. She picked up Tierra's gun and secured it in her own waistband. She looked around to make sure the coast was still clear. Seeing that it was, she stood over Keyz, finding him still breathing and clinging to life. He turned his head sideways and blood frothed from his mouth and ran down the side of his face. Shinette squatted right over him.

"What the hell are you doing?" Tierra was hysterical.

Shinette ignored Tierra and began to insert her gun inside Keyz's mouth. She drew a deep breath, inhaling the celebration of New Year's as it filled the polluted night air.

"Oh my God!" Tierra panted. "What the fuck are you doing? Bitch, let's go!" Tierra's eyes went from Shinette to Keyz who seemed to be in and out of sleep.

Shinette cocked the gun and proceeded to complete their transaction. "Happy New Year's, motherfucker," she said before unleashing the fatal bullet.

Tierra automatically turned her head. She couldn't stomach anymore and began regurgitating right there in the alleyway.

Shinette stood and rushed over to Keyz's car. She snatched the key out of the ignition and went straight for the trunk. When she opened the large black duffle bag that was inside, her heart sank to the pit of her churning stomach. "Shit!"

Tierra nervously wiped the vomit residue on the sleeves of her dress. She turned around and was met with the ill look on Shinette's face. She hurried over to Shinette, her expression changing upon the discovery. She wanted to throw up all over again. The bag full of money they expected to find was not there. Instead, it was full of unmarked dope.

2

"Damn, I wish you would quit with all that leg-shakin' shit!" Shinette blurted. "You fuckin' up my concentration." Shinette was facing the opposite direction, but she could see everything Tierra was doing out of the corner of her eye, and it was pissing her off.

Tierra stopped all at once and crossed one red bottom heel over the other. "Shinette, we just murdered somebody!"

"Your point?" Shinette spat coldly. She continued to fire up the blunt she had just rolled.

"Look, I can't go down for this shit." Tierra's voice cracked with every word. "We said we would only scare him…get the money, and roll out. It wasn't supposed to go down like that!" Tierra's heart burned with fear. She was on edge and couldn't be still. Not even for a minute. She stared into thin air, her head slightly tilted. "Damn…I mean…we killed a man!"

Shinette wrapped her lips around the cigar, inhaled sharply, and held the smoke in her mouth for as long as she could without choking.

Tierra began to cry uncontrollably, causing her mascara to trickle down her flawless apple butter skin. Men would often tell her that she was the prettier of the two, which was primarily the reason she always had the leading role in their heists. She was also the weakest, which was why Shinette always ended up doing the dirty work.

Shinette got up from the mahogany, suede, wingback chair and walked over to where Tierra sat. "You know what? You actin' like a real weak-ass bitch right now! Now it was either that fat dirty motherfucker or us. He would have put a bullet in your head quicker than you can count to one. So why you sitting here grieving over that nigga is beyond me!"

Tierra shook her head solemnly. "I can't go to jail. I can't," she said, thinking about her current situation. Aside from that, jail was not a place she could ever get used to. The six-month stint she had spent in juvenile detention for shoplifting had helped her to realize that she enjoyed her freedom way too much. She clutched her stomach and rocked side to side. More tears poured down her face like a heavy rain.

"Ain't nobody going to jail, T." Shinette took a seat beside her best friend, her ace, her partner in crime. "Look, we in this shit together, all right. You go down, I go down," she said bluntly, as if that would relieve Tierra's worry. "As long as we stick together, we ain't got nothing to worry about. But you can't open your mouth to *nobody* about this. And I mean nobody. Not even yo' nigga."

Tierra gauged the serious look in Shinette's eyes. It was so cold it caused the hairs on the back of her neck to stand up.

"Now we gon' get cleaned up, catch some zees, and as soon as day break, we gone unload these keys." Shinette had already calculated what they could possibly make off the fishscale. As long as Tierra played it cool and didn't crack, everything was going to be fine. Tierra brought her watery eyes to Shinette. Not a word left her lips. Shinette noted her indecisiveness. To erase any doubt Tierra might have had, she asked, "Have I ever been wrong, T?"

Tierra thought long and hard, then slowly shook her head.

"See. So you can trust me on this. I promise you, when it's all said and done, it'll be as good as forgotten." Shinette took one more pull at the blunt before passing it to Tierra. "Here, this'll help you get your mind right." A sinister grin crossed her lips as she grabbed the duffle bag and casually walked off, headed for her bedroom.

Tierra put the cigar out and contemplated on what she should do next.

Once in her room, Shinette tossed the bag on her bed and placed both of the guns on a nearby dresser. She began shedding her blood-soiled clothes, making a note to bag everything and toss it in the Trinity River at sunrise. Her curvaceous petite frame was her greatest asset, and like Tierra, she was built like a stallion. Her perfectly round and firm breasts jiggled as she walked over to her bed to retrieve the remote to her wall-mounted stereo and sixty-inch flat-screen. She powered on both, lowering the volume to the TV.

Shinette and Tierra may have resided in the hood, but they lived like ghetto queens. They had a huge two-bedroom apartment in Pleasant Grove that was lavishly furnished, their closets had all the latest fashion, and Shinette drove a chromed-out whip. They were at the top of their game and Shinette made sure they stayed flossed like the bosses they were. They were constantly on the grind and sometimes money came easy. Way too easy. Robbing fresh on the line corner boys and setting up tricks was their main hustle. Shinette, however, saw it more as a sport. She loved dominating men and got a thrill out of robbing them and taking their money. The more dangerous the heist, the bigger the payoff and the thirstier she became to do it all over again.

She had stashed enough money to chill out on for a year or two, but she couldn't snooze on the latest opportunity that had presented itself. Shinette knew going in that robbing Keyz would set her and Tierra up real nice for the new year. She also knew that killing him would start a street war, right in her own backyard.

Shinette walked over to the mirror and began pinning her hair up like she did every night before her shower. Her callous reaction to tonight's events vindicated that she was in fact built for this. She wasn't remorseful one bit, and if she had to do it all over again, she would have emptied the clip into Keyz and put red lipstick on his lips. She had long ago crowned herself the Greedy Grove Gutta Queen, and it was about time she came out of hiding.

When Rick Ross's "Hold Me Back" came on, she began reciting the rap lyrics and bobbing to the beat. She stopped and almost reached for both of the guns in front of her until she realized it was only Tierra opening her door.

Tierra grimaced at Shinette as if she had never seen her naked before when in fact, she had seen it all, and on more than one occasion. They had engaged in threesomes to set up their targets so seeing her without any clothes should have been normal.

"What's up with it?" Shinette asked, still pinning up her curls and jamming to the music. Not once did she bother asking Tierra why in the hell she was still in those dirty-ass clothes. She figured she was still *processing* everything.

"I'ma chill at Duke's tonight. He's on his way to come get me." Tierra diverted her eyes.

Shinette broke her gaze from the mirror and eyed Tierra suspiciously. "You didn't mention the—"

"No!" Tierra exclaimed, bringing her eyes back to Shinette. "I haven't seen him in a few days and I miss him."

Shinette rolled her eyes upward. "You sick behind a nigga that gave your ass the Clapster?" she chortled. "I guess some bitches never learn."

"Damn, Shinette! Why you always gotta go there and be all up in my personal business like that? Do I keep tabs on what's going on in your panties? *No,* I don't. So I would appreciate it if you kept *my* pussy off *your* mind!"

Shinette pursed her lips. "Tsk. I'm just saying." Her left eyebrow arched. "Your priorities have been a little *fucked up* lately! I'm only being a friend and making sure you don't fall off the damn wagon."

"Well, I don't need you to do shit for me, okay? You've done more than enough. As a matter of fact, after what happened tonight, I'm done with this shit!" Tierra didn't have to give it any more thought. She knew before killing that man tonight that she was getting out of the game, but that was the reason she gave Shinette. This wasn't the kind of life she wanted to continue living. She deserved and wanted more for her and the baby she carried in her stomach.

"Humph. So I guess it's like that?"

"It's getting old, Shinette." Tierra exhaled. "We said we would stop when the shit got outta control." She laid her sympathetic eyes back on her friend's. "It's outta control." Her heart was heavy and she couldn't take it. "We now have a man's blood on our hands."

"All the paper we've made together and you telling me you're ready to bail out because of one little hiccup?" Shinette totally dismissed Tierra's remorseful outcry.

"You call killing a man a fucking hiccup?"

Shinette didn't offer a response, only finished her hair.

"I'm not a fucking murderer! I don't kill people for money!" Tierra kept her eyes on Shinette's. "I'm not trying to die for this shit! I'm better than this."

Shinette calmly walked over to where Tierra stood. "So you think you better than me now?" They were inches apart and Shinette could sense her friend's paranoia. She could hear Tierra's heart racing through her chest and she could smell the fear of an amateur killer. It was almost familiar. When Tierra didn't respond, Shinette simply nodded. "Humph. I see. So that's how it's gon' be from now on? I got it. Well, then roll out. Ain't no-motherfucking-body stopping you!" she spat icily.

Tierra snatched off the blonde wig that she had worn to disguise herself and slung it to the floor. The stocking cap had caused her short, natural wavy hair to frizz up and lose its body.

"I've always had your back," Tierra snapped back, matching Shinette's tone. "But who the fuck gon' have mine if I go down for this?" She didn't wait for Shinette to answer her. Instead, she walked off to go get cleaned up, leaving no room whatsoever for negotiation. That was the end of their discussion.

"I thought you were a chaser, T!" Shinette taunted. "That nigga don't give a fuck about you! Never did. Never will. You wanna bounce? Bounce then! Just remember, I taught you the game! I laced you up! Before I came along you was just another broke-ass welfare candidate looking for a government handout. I'm *your* motherfucking come-up!"

With tears streaming down her face, she took a quick shower, then slipped into a pair of jeggings and a T-shirt. She pulled out one of her small Gucci travel cases and began packing an overnight bag. Shinette's venom-laced words had slaughtered Tierra. Her heart was crushed, and even though she tried to block out everything her friend was saying, it was impossible since it was all true. It was a truth that she couldn't hide from no matter how hard she tried. Shinette had indeed been her Savior. She had given Tierra the game and taught her everything she knew. That was why part of her always felt like she owed Shinette.

At that moment, she began to question if she was doing the

right thing by leaving. But as Duke entered her mind, she thought about her future. Their future. She opened her drawer and took out a white envelope. As she pulled out the contents, she managed a smile. Her right thumb brushed over the black-and-white sonogram image she had gotten two weeks ago at her doctor's appointment. It confirmed she was twelve weeks' pregnant. Tierra had a million reasons for walking out on Shinette, but her unborn baby took precedence over them all. She placed the picture back into the envelope and packed it with the rest of her things. Her heart was heavy, but she had to do what was best for her for a change. She no longer needed Shinette and it was about time she proved it.

It wasn't until she was in the confines of Duke's two-story house that Tierra truly felt safe. He lived more than an hour away from the city in a nice secluded suburb. Whenever Tierra went over, it felt like home. It was where she wanted to be. Where she needed to be. And to think she had almost allowed Shinette to convince her into breaking it off with him. Tierra was starting to believe that Shinette had been jealous of her and Duke's relationship all along. Duke took care of her to the highest degree. She didn't have to hustle. He bought her any and everything she wanted and took her wherever she wanted to go. It was the first time ever in her life that a man treated her like a queen and with respect.

Tierra faced Duke. The essence of their sweet lovemaking still trapped between the sheets. While Duke put it on her the way she liked it, with her unsettled thoughts, Tierra wouldn't have known the difference. What she did know was that she was right where she wanted to be—in his arms. His chocolate brown eyes melted into hers as he traced her lips before leaning in to kiss her again.

"Do you love me?" Tierra asked finally, needing the reassurance from him now more than ever.

Duke drew his neck back, completely caught off-guard by her question. "Of course I do, babe. Why you asking me a question you should already know the answer to?" He studied her glowing hazel eyes.

Tierra inhaled deeply, feeling it was the perfect time to tell him about the baby. She had thought long and hard all week about where, when, and how she would tell him. He had a right to know that his seed was growing inside of her belly. She had no doubt in her mind that Duke would make a good father. He was loving, supportive, and a provider. And although he had a warehouse job, Tierra knew without a shadow of a doubt that he would work his fingers to the bone to ensure her and the baby were okay. She ended the conference she was having with herself and determined it was time. He deserved to know everything. Even if it meant betraying her best friend. Her loyalty to Shinette and her love for Duke became a mental battle the longer she stared into his eyes.

"I'm asking…" Tierra paused and wiped the tears forming in the pockets of her eyes.

"Talk to me, babe." Duke's brows furrowed and a worrisome look washed over his face.

She diverted her eyes before finding the strength she needed to go through with this. "I did something very bad tonight." Tierra's bottom lip began to quiver. More tears collected on her face, somehow managing to clog her throat during their transition.

Duke placed his arm around her warm body. The pained look on Tierra's face was one he had never seen before. "Come on now, baby. It couldn't have been that bad." He continuously wiped away her tears. "Everything's going to be okay. I'm here."

Duke's words hardly comforted Tierra like they would have normally, and as his large soft hands circled her back, her mind began to replay the events. Each image more vivid than before. As her swelling eyes began to burn and her head began to pound, Tierra stared at Duke with a now clouded vision. The words that followed were barely audible. As if she didn't want God himself to hear her admit to what she had done that night.

"I killed a man," Tierra confessed.

Duke's eyes bucked and he rose completely from the covers, scooting his back against the six-foot-tall, wooden headboard. He swallowed hard and cleared his throat. "You did what?" he asked, looking at Tierra a little differently.

His reaction didn't surprise Tierra. Only confirmed what was at risk. She hesitated before continuing, feeling as if the air in the room was suddenly beginning to suffocate her.

"Shinette and I killed a man tonight."

Duke eyed her incredulously as he tried to force his heart to override what was going through his mind. Every muscle in his body stiffened, temporarily paralyzing him. As more tears piled on Tierra's face, Duke knew that his duty was to console her. But she had dropped one helluva bombshell on him, making it close to impossible to keep a level head. He sighed deeply as his thoughts took him in circles. It was that quickly that everything he thought he knew about the woman in front of him, vanished.

"What happened?" Duke asked, finding it difficult not to judge her.

"I...didn't mean to do it," Tierra proclaimed. She sat up in the bed. "It just happened so fast. It was either him or us," she cried frantically. She struggled to breathe. "Shinette had been planning this money gig for five months now. I was going to stop after this one," she cried. Her words began to fall apart. "Oh my God. And now a man is dead." She took a moment to gather her thoughts, shaking her head as the gory image of Keyz reappeared in her mind. Tierra lifted her hands. "I have a man's blood on my hands!"

Duke rocked Tierra in his arms as she poured out every bloody detail. She confided in him about all the other licks she and Shinette had hit in the past several weeks. Months. Years. She explained to Duke how it had been their hustle and way of survival. He listened intently. Never saying a word. Tierra stopped talking as she watched Duke's face tighten. She had hoped he wouldn't judge her, but she felt that was exactly what he was doing. Fear, intertwined with her gullible mindset, had Tierra divulging her deepest and darkest secrets. All but the one that included him—his baby.

"So did anybody see y'all tonight?" Duke asked finally.

Tierra shook her head.

"It's going to be all right." Duke kissed her on the forehead. "In the meantime, I want you to stay here with me."

His words sounded more like lullabies to Tierra's ears. "Okay, baby," she replied weakly, yawning simultaneously. Her eyes grew heavier and before she knew it, she had drifted off to sleep.

3

"Where's this bitch at?" Shinette huffed. She had been calling Tierra all morning long and hadn't been able to get a hold of her. She started to leave another message but disconnected the call instead. She was hoping that she could talk some sense into her, but with or without her, Shinette was determined to flip last night's dope inheritance by any means necessary. In the back of her mind, Tierra would soon come crawling back once she realized the real. Game recognized game and if Tierra wasn't so dick-whipped, she would have been able to see everything that Shinette had been trying to warn her about.

All this time Shinette thought she had schooled Tierra on this street life. *Money Over Niggas* had been their hood motto and they vowed they would never let a man come between them and their paper chase. It was a pact they had formed in the very beginning. Shinette had instilled in Tierra that every man was to be treated as a prospect—a potential lick. They used every ounce of their game to manipulate men and swindle them out of their money. And when that didn't work, they straight up robbed their asses. One way or another they had to come up off the loot.

Coasting on the memories of how tight they used to be, Shinette sadly took another hit of her blunt and chalked it up to Tierra's denseness. "Some hoes get bit by the dick. That hoe got swallowed,"

Shinette guffawed as she pursed her lips and exhaled a cloud of smoke.

She slipped her cell phone back into her purse and brought her morning ritual to an abrupt end. She grabbed the duffle bag off the dining room table and headed out the door, dressed to kill in a black sleek, V-neck halter dress and five-inch heels. Her voluminous ebony curls were loosely pulled together and draped over her right shoulder. She took long strides across the parking lot all the way to her car.

Coasting along I-30 East, blasting Rick Ross, Shinette drove five miles under the speed limit. The state troopers were hot this time of day and she didn't want to give them any reason to pull her over, especially since she was only fifteen minutes away from her destination. She glanced over at the bag in the passenger's seat. Her hands began to itch from the mere thought of the money she was about to make from the swap. She lowered the sun visor and checked herself in the mirror. Yep, she looked good enough to eat.

Tierra woke to the sound of voices coming from downstairs. She heard Duke and another man talking over one another. She lay in bed for a moment longer, straining her ears and trying to make out what they were saying. Her attempts were useless. She squinted her tired eyes at the radio clock. It was 11:21 a.m. She had clearly overslept.

Feeling the sudden urge to pee, she hopped out of bed, naked, and made a beeline for the bathroom. The events from the night before came crashing down on her before she could even relieve herself. Tierra tried to block out the flashing images that burned in her mind, but couldn't. She could almost smell Keyz's decomposing corpse as if she were still there in that alley. She could see his fluttering eyelids fighting to stay open as life deserted him. Tierra woke up this morning a murderer, and no matter where she ran or hid, she could never escape what she and Shinette had done.

Tierra jacked up the toilet lid and lowered her face over the bowl. She began to regurgitate. Shortly after that, the queasy feeling swarming inside of her stomach subsided. She grabbed a towel from the linen closet and walked over to the sink. She turned on the cold water, then cupped her hands under the stream. She dipped her head into the sink and splashed her face repeatedly. She took some water into her mouth, swished it around, and spat it back into the sink. She finally stared at the woman in the mirror, hardly recognizing her. This killer. Unable to stand the sight of herself any longer, she hopped into the tub and showered for almost an hour.

The cold hardwood squeaked beneath Tierra's feet as she retreated back to the bedroom. She no longer heard Duke and his company. She figured they'd both left. She walked over to the window anyway and peered out the shutters. Duke's work van was parked in the driveway next to his Audi. Knowing he was still home brought Tierra some relief. She rubbed her stomach as she walked over to the chair where her purse was and retrieved her cell phone. She had several missed calls and text messages. All were from Shinette. She scrolled over each text until she came to the last one that read: *MONEY OVER NIGGAS!* Tierra shook her head, disgusted that Shinette could even be thinking about money at a time like this. Shinette proved to be just as heartless and cutthroat as she always boasted to be. Tierra instantly began deleting the messages, and as she was doing so, her phone started to ring. Tierra didn't recognize the number but answered anyway.

"Hello," Tierra said apprehensively.

"Damn, it's like that now. I gotta call you from a different number in order for you to answer your phone?" Shinette asked coolly.

Tierra rolled her eyes. Shinette was the *last* person she wanted to speak to. "Look, we don't have nothing to talk about," she quipped.

Shinette couldn't believe that after all she'd done for Tierra, this was how she repaid her. She gave her a place to lay her head when no one else did. Took her under her wings and even taught the bitch how to fly. Duke had done exactly what she suspected he would. He had come between their friendship. Anger danced in Shinette's eyes. This was cutting her deep.

"You know what," Shinette began. "I've always looked out for you. I treated you like you were my motherfucking blood and you gon' play me like this! That pussy hoe over there can't save you. You the side bitch, dummy!"

Tierra shook her head, predicting where the conversation was headed. She cut Shinette off before she could go any further. "I already told you what I had to say so you can quit—"

"It's that hoe-ass nigga, isn't it?" Shinette blurted out of nowhere. "Your head is so far up his nut sac, you shitting peanuts!"

"Fuck you! This ain't about Duke so leave him out of it. This is between *you* and *me!*"

A devious smirk on her face, Shinette allowed her words to marinate her tongue before their long and overdue exit. "See, that's where you're wrong again. This *is* about your man." With that, Shinette ended the call.

Tierra held the phone in her hand a minute longer before realizing that Shinette had hung up in her face. That last remark left a bitter taste in her mouth, but she was too wrapped up in her own thoughts to entertain Shinette's bullshit. "Who was that?" Duke asked, causing Tierra to jump at the sound of his deep voice. Unbeknownst to Tierra, he had overheard parts of her conversation.

Tierra turned around to face Duke who looked even sexier in the morning. He was dressed casually in solid black jeans and a black wife beater that exposed his tattoo sleeves. His presence always brought a smile to her face.

"You scared me." Tierra smiled as she wrapped her hands loosely around his neck, kissing him on his mahogany lips.

Duke relaxed his shoulders and smiled. "My bad, baby."

"I thought you had to work today."

"Called in. Family emergency."

Tierra's face lit up. "Awww...you didn't have to call in for me, baby."

Duke wore his handsome charismatic smile so well. Too well. "Who'd you say that was again?"

"Nobody but Shinette."

Duke looked past Tierra's innocent face and saw nothing but a stone-cold killer. He didn't sleep a wink last night and it was all because of her. Tierra had dropped so much on him that not everything registered until four-thirty this morning when he received a phone call from one of his workers, informing him that he had been robbed, and that his cousin, Keyz, had been murdered. His body had been found in an alley. Duke wanted to die when he received the news. He and Keyz were like brothers. In fact, they called each other brothers. They were raised and brought up in the same home, and when they got older, they moved out and began doing exactly what they saw Duke's father do—hustle. The only difference between the two cousins was that Duke had chosen to maintain a legitimate lifestyle and stay low-key. He allowed Keyz and his other workers to run his drug operations while he worked full-time as a warehouse manager for a roofing company that paid minimum wage compared to his side hustle. But it served its purpose and kept the Feds off his back.

Duke hated getting his hands dirty unless it was absolutely necessary, and now, it was that time. With as many henchmen he had working for him, it wouldn't be hard to track down Keyz's killer. At least that was his immediate thought when he got the call. Lucky for him, he wouldn't have to ride out for this one. Nah, this one would be easy, and he wouldn't even have to leave his house.

So as Tierra looked up at him smiling, her glowing face more beautiful than ever, Duke's racing thoughts made him uneasy. He contemplated pulling out the .45 automatic tucked in his waist and blowing her brains out right then and there to get it over with. He'd send that pretty little bullet crashing through her temple without an ounce of remorse. Unlike Tierra, he was no rookie.

The longer he stood there premeditating his girlfriend's murder, Duke realized this situation was slightly different than any other. In the short time he'd known Tierra, he'd caught feelings for her. Feelings that he had never had for any chick. This was the exact reason why he had vowed to never put all his trust in a female. But Tierra played him good. He thought she was different from all the other ratchet broads he'd ever fucked with. Duke couldn't believe how bad he had slipped up; it could have easily been him getting bagged. He had trusted Tierra and allowed her into his home. She knew where he laid his head. That was mistake number one.

Duke brought their now meaningless tongue kiss to a halt. He needed more information. It was time to find out exactly what all Tierra knew.

"So what home-girl want so early in the damn morning?"

Tierra stepped back and walked over to the bed with Duke following closely behind.

She pursed her lips. "Giving me hell about being here. The usual."

Duke watched her like a hawk. "Oh yeah. So, what'd you tell her?"

"Psst. I told her that I didn't have shit to say to her."

"After what went down last night, I'm sure she's not trying to hear that." Duke stood directly in front of Tierra. "She might be over there flipping out. I mean...I'm sure she scared too. We might need to go check on her. Make sure she's okay and everything." His eyes narrowed, trained on Tierra and her every move.

"Hell no! We're not going back there. Besides, she's not even at home. Right about now, she's probably out flipping that package." Tierra buried her head into her hands, then exhaled. As thoughtful as Duke was, she was not dragging him into her and Shinette's bullshit. It was already bad enough that her hands were dirty. She could have been a wanted woman right now for all she knew. For once in their relationship, she was going to protect him.

Duke sat down beside Tierra and placed his arm around her waist. "Well, no matter what happens, I'm here for you. But I have a gut feeling that everything's going to be all right," he said soothingly.

Tierra raised her head. "How can you be so sure?"

"Because your man got your back. I'm all the protection you need, baby."

When Tierra smiled this time, her dimples were more pronounced. She desperately needed to hear those words, but she could only hope Duke was right. Facing him with the truth about her wasn't easy. He wasn't happy with what he had learned about her, but he didn't judge her either. That was why she loved him.

"I have something else I need to tell you."

Duke's chest tightened as memories of his cousin began to intercept his original thoughts. He had fallen into a daydream as Tierra's lips moved in slow motion.

"I know we've been on and off for two years now...can't say that we've *always* had our shit together. But I think we've both matured and we're ready to take things to another level." She took a deep breath and before she could start up again, Duke's cell started ringing.

"Hold that thought, baby," he said, rising from the bed. Duke pulled his phone out of his pocket and answered it. He remained in the room but walked far enough away from Tierra so that she couldn't hear the exchange on the other end of the line.

"I'm in," the caller reported.

Duke's true feelings were inconspicuous. He had reserved his reprisal for later. "Good work," he rattled off. "Now take out the trash," he added, giving his most loyal goon clearance to eradicate their enemy.

"Say no more, Boss. Time to toe tag this motherfucker!" he said before disconnecting the call.

Duke eased his phone back in his pocket and walked over to Tierra. While he was on his call, she had been thinking that maybe it really wasn't time for her to tell him about the baby. She took all the distractions and interruptions as a warning sign.

"Now what were you about to tell me?" Duke asked, taking his place back beside her on the edge of the bed.

She slowly licked her lips and crawled over his lap. She tried her best to push everything to the back of her mind. "I was going to tell you how much I love you," she lied, kissing him with more passion than before. She lifted his shirt from over his head and tossed it behind them.

Duke picked her up and changed positions. She automatically scooted to the center of the bed, knowing what time it was. He dropped his pants, climbed on top of her, and began rubbing on her hairless pussy, causing it to gush. She moaned in delight, begging him to put it in. He parted her legs some more and eased inside of her. Tierra let out a stricken gasp as he plunged deeper into her, hitting all the right spots. The sound of his gun being cocked was completely drowned out by the propelling of his arousal, and her cries of pleasure. Duke's large fingers snaked along her neck, applying slight pressure with every thrust. He lowered his head and sucked roughly on her breasts, biting down on her thick nipples to incite another round of moans. Their bodies made music. It felt good and bad. So good that Tierra called out his name at the brink of her climax, not realizing for one second that her life was about to end.

Duke took Tierra there, but his mind was too far gone to even come close to reaching an orgasm. He was surprised he was even able to get an erection despite all the madness in his mind. The longer Duke lay on top of her, inside of her, the harder it became for him to pull the trigger and blow the back of her brains out the way she had done his cousin.

With his left hand camped under the pillow where the gun rested, he began stroking her chin with the other hand. Her lips latched onto his and he responded with what he knew would be that fatal kiss.

4

Shinette constantly glanced out of her rearview mirror as she made a right onto her street. She had no reason to believe anyone was following her, but in her line of business, there was no room for error. She refused to get caught slipping. That was why her guard stayed up.

She lowered the volume on the music as she pulled into her apartment complex, circling it three times before finally parking in her designated spot. She checked the rearview again and the side mirrors before reaching for the bag in the passenger seat. As she got out of the car, Shinette couldn't help but feel like she had robbed a bank and had escaped with $75,000 cold hard cash. That's how smooth her latest transaction had gone. There was only one person in the world who could get her a fast turnaround on that many bricks in such short notice, and that happened to be her mother's ex-boyfriend, Kenneth. He was one of the dirtiest cops that ever existed. She never understood what her mother ever saw in him. On second thought, she did. Money.

Shinette had taken a major loss, because in actuality, the five keys combined were worth well over $100,000. But time was of the essence, so the quicker she unloaded them, the quicker she could get the fuck out of dodge and lay low for a minute.

She had contemplated leaving Texas for the longest time, and with all the money she had saved, along with today's earnings, she could leave and never look back if she wanted to. She and Tierra had infiltrated so many dope dealers' trap spots that it was only a matter of time before they got caught. Leaving now was not only the best move for business, but it was a smart move if she wanted to stay alive. Besides, Texas was dried up like the Atacama Desert. It was time to explore new opportunities.

Shinette walked hastily toward her unit. She could hear those bad-ass kids that lived on the first floor, running around like they'd lost their minds. She took to the steps. She was still bothered by how Tierra had gone sour on her. Before speaking with Tierra today, Shinette had every intention on splitting the money, but after her fly-ass mouth, she wasn't getting a penny.

Shinette moved at a more eager pace than before once she made it to the top floor. Her mind was made up. She would move all her things into storage first thing tomorrow and be on the first plane gassed up for Las Vegas. She entered her apartment, placed the bag on the living room couch, and kicked off her heels. She had worn the attire especially for Kenneth who always had the hots for her since she was sixteen. Today, she used his perverted ass to her advantage. He took all the weight off her hand without charging her a handling fee, whereas that same transaction would have cost her a few grand in applicable street taxes. But Kenneth wanted the pussy so bad that he was willing to sacrifice a profit to get it.

Walking instinctively straight to Tierra's room, Shinette opened her closet. All of her clothes were still hanging there. She pulled out her drawers. Everything was still folded the same way she had left them. Shinette checked Tierra's bathroom. Her toothbrush was still in its holder; her $30 face bar was still in the box; the Guilty Gucci perfume was exactly where she'd always kept it.

Nothing of Tierra's was out of place, which could have only meant one thing.

Shinette retreated to her own bedroom. She turned on the television and stereo. She raised the volume and headed for the bathroom. Once inside, she eased the door shut and walked over to the tub. She plugged the drain and turned up the hot water for the shower. Instead of getting inside the tub, she pulled the curtain closed. Shinette took off all her clothes, leaving them strewn on the center of the floor. Soon as the wide mounted mirror exposing her nudity began to fog, she slipped behind the door.

Less than two minutes later, the bathroom door slowly crept open, as Shinette had anticipated. A bare outstretched hand graced a heavy piece of hardware. She was as quiet as a roach. The assailant silently snuck past her, unbeknownst of her position. He was unmasked and dressed in true goon fashion from his head down to his feet. His black and long wavy hair was pulled back in a single ponytail, allowing Shinette to get a close look at the bold cursive lettering tattooed on the right side of his neck. She was able to make out a woman's name, underneath it, "rest in peace." She pressed her lips tightly together knowing that whomever the woman was, she would soon have company.

Shinette and the intruder were merely an arm's length distance from each other. She could almost hear his heart tick. His calm slow breaths, confident stance, and direct headshot aim, led her to believe that this wasn't his first time. Like her, he wasn't afraid to catch another body. He had come prepared to execute his mission, and the closer he got to the tub, the tighter Shinette's right hand folded around her Nina. She held her breath, ready to spray at any given moment and light his ass up like a Mexican Christmas tree. She didn't blink once for fear he'd hear it. The steam building in the air had obscured her so well she could no longer see her reflection. Yet her eyes never lost sight of this dead man walking. His fate had already been sealed long before he woke this morning. However, Shinette was going to do the honors of deliverance.

The gun leveled in his right hand, he blindly aimed at what he had hoped was Shinette's head. The instant he reached to pull back the curtain with the other hand, Shinette let loose a double that reverberated off the bathroom walls. Blood splattered everything in plain sight. He caught the first slug in the middle of his spine and the other in his right shoulder—the last hit forcing him to drop his gun in the tub full of water.

He managed to turn around before slowly dropping to the floor, pulling the shower curtain and the rod down with him. He groaned in agonizing pain as he stared wide-eyed at the naked being standing over him. He placed his bloody hand on the edge of the tub and tried pulling himself up until gravity forced him right back down. He looked down drunkenly at his shirt and began to panic at the sight of his own blood.

"Agggghhh!" he groaned as he tried to scoot as far away from Shinette as he could.

Shinette watched on as his shirt became drenched with blood. She squatted next to him, reducing herself to his level. "Who the fuck sent you?" she seethed. The icy glare he gave her didn't rattle her one bit. "Who the *fuck* sent you?" Her interrogation seemed to be getting her nowhere.

He let out a loose chuckle and scathingly retorted, "Bitch, I ain't telling you a damn thing." He unleashed a glob of spit dead in the center of her face. "Now use that to suck my dick!"

Shinette snapped, and before she could think twice, she rammed the gun to his temple and let it sing. She didn't give her finger a break until she heard the click, indicating that there were no bullets left. What was left of his head, slumped forward. Blood was splattered everywhere and spewed from every single hole she'd put in his body. She jumped up and rushed to the sink to wash all the blood and spittle from her face and neck. When she was finished, she walked back over to his lifeless body. She rummaged through his left pocket, pulling out the very piece of evidence that had given him away—Newport cigarettes. Although he didn't light the cigarette in her house, the distinctive stench in his clothes along with his musky cologne had left a trail. Shinette reached into his other pocket and pulled out his cell phone, ID card, an unopened pack of condoms, and a single door key. She stared at the key long and hard. Unless it was a coincidence that he liked pink butterflies, there was only one other person to whom that key could have belonged. That one little key explained why Tierra was acting the way that she had that morning. Shinette didn't want to believe how this was even possible, but as she stared down at the man she had decapitated, she understood better than anybody else that when shit got dirty, somebody had to clean it up. Although she never would have guessed in a million years that her own best friend would have ordered the hit. But unlike her, Tierra was too soft to do the job herself so she had to send a punk-ass bitch to do her job.

Shinette's psychotic mindset took her everywhere. She didn't like the feeling that began to fill her gut, but it was obvious to her that Tierra was a traitor. She had double-crossed Shinette and then tried to have her killed.

Shinette turned off the water and stepped around Jason Hamilton's corpse. She jetted to her bedroom and quickly slipped on a pair of jeans and an oversized T-shirt. She snatched clothes off hangers, gathering only enough to fill her bag. With no time to spare, she ran through the living room, grabbed the bag of money, and dashed out the door. Her heart raced as she rushed down the steps, worried that someone might have reported the shots. She didn't look back, only picked up her pace.

She opened her car door and immediately tossed the bags in the backseat. She started the engine and peeled off through the parking lot, only slowing down when she got to the gate. It seemed to take forever to open and when it did, she nearly floored the car's accelerator. Pulling out of the complex and entering a flow of traffic, she saw two Dallas squad cars racing in the opposite direction. She looked in her rearview and saw that they had turned into her apartment complex. She had made it out just in time. She respired and made a quick right, headed for the interstate.

5

There was a smothering silence that floated in Duke's bedroom. He sat on the edge of the bed, his head buried in the palm of his hands. Tierra's desperate pleas for help were trapped behind the rag he had stuffed in her mouth right before taping it shut. A bucket of tears poured freely down her face and her eyes begged for mercy. She bucked her head violently, straining every vein in her neck as she tried to shake free from the restraints. Duke had tied her hands and feet to the chair with cable wire, practically cutting off her circulation. She strained herself to the point she peed herself.

Duke was out of his head and the longer he delayed killing Tierra, the more he began to care that she was carrying his seed. She had blurted out that she was pregnant right as his finger prepared to pull the trigger. He was ready to avenge the death of his cousin, Keyz, and do to her what he would have done to any nigga in the street. Being a bitch didn't mean she was exempt from catching that fire. When it was all said and done, he didn't give a damn about the dope. All he wanted was Tierra and Shinette dead, and their bodies dumped in the landfill along with the rest of the trash.

Now, Duke wrestled with the fact that if Tierra was indeed pregnant, he would be killing his own baby as well. That thought alone sent him over the edge. He jumped up from the bed, walked straight over to where she was and slapped her so hard her neck popped.

Tierra's entire face turned red and blood trickled from her nose. She couldn't even feel the left side of her face any longer. She squeezed her eyes tight and jerked wildly.

"Y'all killed my fucking blood!" Duke got up in her face. He placed the muzzle of the gun directly on Tierra's forehead. "Bitch, I should just do you in right motherfucking now! How the fuck I know it's mine?" he hollered. "Matter fact, how the fuck do I know you even pregnant?"

Tierra blinked her eyes constantly, her only means of communicating to him.

Duke yanked off the tape and snatched the rag out of her mouth. She immediately began throwing up and coughing simultaneously. When she was able to catch her breath, she hollered, "Help!" at the top of her lungs.

"Ain't nobody gonna hear your rabbit ass!"

"Please don't kill me," Tierra begged of him as globs of bloody snob ran down her mouth. "This is your baby! I promise it's yours." Her breathing became heavy as she tried to inhale as much air possible before he gagged her again. "Please, Duke. I didn't mean to hurt you," she cried. When she saw that he wasn't responding, she yelled again. "Help!"

Duke rammed the gun into her mouth, shoving it past her teeth. "Scream one more damn time and I'll splatter your brains all over this fucking wall!"

"Agwwwah..." Tierra wailed, knowing he would make good on his threat. It was written all over his face. Everything before an hour ago had been a mystery until Duke revealed that the man she and Shinette had murdered, was his cousin. Duke then began accusing her of trying to set him up too. The more he talked, the quicker she began to tie everything together, realizing that the set-up from the night before had all been a part of Shinette's plan from day one. Tierra had no idea that Duke was a major drug dealer, and while Shinette had insinuated that Duke wasn't to be trusted, Tierra had written it off as jealousy. It didn't register that Shinette was trying to expose him. But greed had also set in during that process. Shinette had used Tierra's relationship with Duke to her advantage, making it that much easier for her to keep tabs on Duke and his drug operations, all with the intent of robbing him right under their noses. Shinette had outsmarted them both.

Duke yanked the gun back.

"I'm sorry," Tierra pleaded. "Please believe me...I...I didn't know he was your cousin."

"Bitch, don't give me that! And you can kill all the fake-ass theatrics." Duke pulled back. "You and that hoe knew exactly what y'all were doing! Y'all set this whole thing up and now you expect me to believe that you didn't know he was my kinfolk? What the fuck I look like believing your trifling ass! You didn't think I would figure this shit out?"

Tierra couldn't believe how Duke had turned on her. It all felt like a horrible nightmare. "But what about our baby, Duke? Please. I'm begging you. I promise we can fix this," she told him. "Think about our baby!"

Duke's face twisted into a scowl. "There ain't shit to fix." He balled up the rag and gagged her once again. "You better start saying your prayers because when I get back, your life is going to be riding on your piss."

Duke walked out of the room, headed to buy a pregnancy test. If Tierra wasn't pregnant, he was going to murk her ass before her piss could dry on the stick. He pressed the button on his key-ring to unlock his car and as he got ready to walk out of the door, he remembered his wallet was on the kitchen counter. He walked hastily to the back of the house to retrieve it.

The instant he got inside his car and closed the door, his phone started going off. He pulled it from his pocket. Seeing that it was Jason's number, he anxiously pressed TALK.

"Man, you handle that bitch?" Duke asked as he started up the engine.

"Yeah, I handled that bitch!" Shinette sprung up from behind him. Before he knew what was coming, she hooked one arm around his head and pulled it toward her chest, using all her strength. Duke was blindly grabbing for her head, but before he could get his hands high enough in the air, Shinette drove the knife deep into his flesh, slicing his throat from ear to ear.

Blood sprayed out of Duke's neck. He immediately placed both hands around his throat, trying to apply enough pressure to stop the profuse bleeding. His efforts were futile. He was hemorrhaging to death. His jugular vein and carotid artery had been severed in one swipe before he knew what had hit him. Gurgling sounds escaped Duke as he tried to hold on to dear life.

Quivering in shock, he widened his unbelieving eyes as he watched himself die at the hands of a bitch. Staring back at him in the rearview mirror was Shinette in full gorilla gutta form with a black ski mask covering her face. A weak shrill lifted off his throat but crashed before it could reach his ears. Duke started to lose oxygen. The loud thumping of his heartbeat sounded more like a trumpet, serenading him to a state of unconsciousness as he drowned seemingly in a sea of his own blood. Shinette completely emerged from the backseat. It was only a matter of minutes before the Grim Reaper came to claim his soul. She leaned over and pulled the keys from the ignition, dropping Jason's phone in Duke's lap. "Pussy nigga!" she bantered. She slipped out of the car and started straight for the house. She walked through the front door, gun cocked and ready. She was looking for the one person who she knew had set her up.

Shinette didn't hear a peep, which kept her on her toes. She walked through the entire downstairs and there was no Tierra in sight. She took to the stairs, climbing them slowly and quietly. Once she reached the top, she looked down over the banister. She believed she was imagining things when she heard what sounded like muffled screams.

She moved in the direction of the noise, her finger gracing the trigger. She was prepared to shoot anything moving. Her heels clawed at the hardwood floors, announcing her presence on her behalf. She pushed the bedroom door completely open and to her surprise, Tierra was butt-ass naked, gagged, and strapped to a chair.

Fear consumed Tierra once the masked intruder entered the room. The thoughts that charged her, forced her to accept that Duke had sent someone to finish her off. He must have loved her too much to carry it out himself. Trapped between what was actually happening and fearing the unknown, left Tierra completely restless. She tried to convince herself that death would be easier, but the thought of her unborn baby not having a chance at life, revitalized her. Tears flowed like pouring rain down her cheeks as she jerked uncontrollably.

Shinette analyzed the situation, only to reach one conclusion. It wasn't Tierra that had sent Jason to kill her, it was Duke. He had stolen Tierra's key and sent his goon after her. But how could Duke have known that they were the ones who killed Keyz and robbed him? She shook her head. The missing piece to the puzzle instantly revealed itself. Tierra had sold Shinette out like the traitor she had become. She had told Duke all about the lick they hit, not realizing that she was in fact, running her mouth to the one they had robbed.

Shinette walked closer to Tierra who she now deemed useless. She had become nothing more than a liability and a lost cause. A snitch bitch. Once Tierra recognized who the assailant was underneath the ski mask, she froze. Confusion registered on her face, but she knew that Shinette had come to her rescue. Her prayers had been answered. She began to breathe in relief until the gun Shinette held at her side, lifted midway in the air. Before Tierra knew it, she was staring down the barrel of her own gun. The gun that had Keyz's dead body attached to it.

Shinette slowly pulled the rag out of Tierra's mouth.

"Shinette, what are you doing?" Tierra immediately asked.

Not a single word left Shinette's lips. She stared at Tierra through the eyes of a serial killer. Neither of them would have been in this predicament if Tierra had not opened her damn mouth. If she had only listened to Shinette, things would not have to end this way. Tierra had proven that she couldn't be trusted, and if she betrayed Shinette once, she'd betray her again.

"I'm sorry...please...," Tierra begged for her life.

Shinette pointed the gun at Tierra's heaving chest.

"No! Don't do this. Please...please...please...my baby...please..."

Tears formed in Shinette's eyes. She didn't want to do what she was about to do, but she had to deal with this now, or risk everything. By nightfall, Duke's goons would be gunning for them both. Better Tierra catch that bullet than her. "I'm begging you! I don't want to die! Please..."

"I love you," Shinette squeezed out right before the gun went off.

Tierra sucked in a large amount of air as soon as the bullet tore through her heart. She got one last look at Shinette before her eyelids folded over the whites of her eyes. It wasn't long after that before her heart stopped beating.

Shinette removed the ski mask and closed her grief-stricken eyes, unable to bear the sight of her dead friend. She placed the gun near Tierra's feet. She walked out of that room and did not look back.

Shinette raced down the steps. She had to get out of there. She sorted through Duke's keys until she found the one to unlock his work truck. She hopped inside and drove half a mile up the road where she had parked her car. She moved swiftly as she transferred the bags into the truck. The farther she got from the crime scene the better off, she would be. She headed straight for the Dallas-Fort Worth Airport. She would lay low for a while, but she'd be back. Dallas was home, and after all, she was the Greedy Grove Gutta Queen. But until her return, she was going to continue to do what she did best. *CHASE!*

N'Tyse is the erotic romance author of several bestselling novels. She is also executive producer and director of the documentary film, Beneath My Skin. *While N'Tyse, pronounced entice, spells out exotic seduction, the true significance behind her name takes on an entire new meaning. The acronym translates to* Never Tell Your Secret*—a message she envelops within her stimulating taboo tales.*

The author's passion for writing dates back to a very young age where she found poetry, music, and creative writing as an outlet. In 2007 N'Tyse ambitiously penned and self-published her freshman and sophomore novels, My Secrets Your Lies *and* Stud Princess Notorious Vendettas, *which went on to grace many bestseller lists, including* The Dallas Morning Newspaper.

N'Tyse currently juggles her writing career as a full-time mom, wife, and documentary filmmaker. She is the author of Twisted Seduction *and* Twisted Vows of Seduction. *Her literary contributions have been featured in magazines and several bestselling anthologies, including* Zane Presents Purple Panties 2: Missionary No More, *and Zane's* Z-Rated: Chocolate Flava

3. *N'Tyse currently resides in Dallas, Texas where she is hard at work on the next installment in her Twisted series. Vist the author at www.ntyse.com; www.facebook.com/author.ntyse; www.twitter.com/ntyse; ntyse.amillionthoughts@yahoo.com*

If you liked "Chasers," be sure to check out N'Tyse's full-length novels. Enjoy this taste of

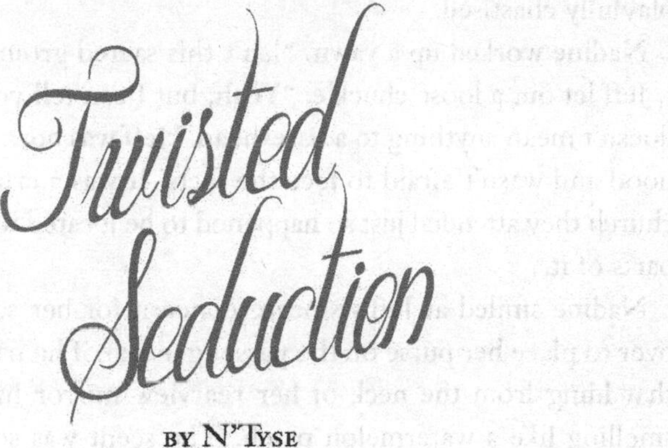

Twisted Seduction

by N'Tyse

Available from Strebor Books

1

Three years earlier

It was so dark and windy that night. Nadine planned on leaving right after choir rehearsal and heading straight home because she had an early morning briefing with Denise, her business partner and best friend, and the rest of their staff. They were going to discuss a strategy to save the $6 million dollar portfolio they were in danger of losing to the bank.

The car alarm to Nadine's Inuit white Audi made a chirping sound when she pressed the keyless entry remote to deactivate it. Just as she got ready to open her door, Jeff Jackson, Denise's husband, appeared out of nowhere with his arm graciously extended in Nadine's direction.

"Here, let me get that for you," Jeff offered, stepping in front of

Nadine before she could reach for the door handle. "Woman, you know better than to come out here all by yourself while it's this dark," he playfully chastised.

Nadine worked up a yawn. "Isn't this sacred ground?"

Jeff let out a loose chuckle. "Yeah, but I can tell you right now that doesn't mean anything to a base-head." Jeff was born and raised in the hood and wasn't afraid to face the facts. It was a cruel world and the church they attended just so happened to be located in one of the worst parts of it.

Nadine smiled at Jeff's sincere concern for her safety. She leaned over to place her purse on the passenger seat. The fruity air freshener that hung from the neck of her rearview mirror had the entire car smelling like a watermelon patch. The scent was so strong, Nadine instantly regretted choosing it over the jasmine floral deodorizer she normally bought. She slowly turned back around to face a tower of smooth and handsome dark chocolate. Jeff was well dressed as always, wearing a black, two-button, single-breasted suit jacket; underneath it a white French-fly dress shirt. Blue denim instead of dress pants. Nadine never thought a pair of jeans could look so damn good on a man. She struggled to keep her gaze from settling on Jeff's lower half, allowing her eyes to take in his large white patent leather Jordans; at least a size twelve in her estimation. Not only did Jeff have a natural swagger, he had a sense of style, too. Old school flava with New Age spunk and looks that could conjure the panties right off a woman.

Nadine's eyes hungrily examined him from head to toe. Something was missing and then it hit her at once; his glasses. With the bit of light from her car, she was able to look straight into his mesmerizing chestnut-brown eyes.

"Where's Denise?" she inquired finally. "I thought she'd be here tonight." She pushed her hair behind her ears. It never failed. Every time she found herself in Jeff's presence, she grew nervous. Out of the six years she'd known him, that butterfly feeling still swarmed around the pit of her stomach, holding her accountable for all of her woulda-coulda-shouldas.

Jeff folded his arms. "I don't know where my wife is. She said she needed to take care of some things at the office and then she'd be heading over afterwards, but"—Jeff scoffed as he looked around the empty parking lot—"I guess we can see she never got around to it. So she has me running her errands." He raised a stack of Christmas programs bound together with a thick rubber band. But even if Denise hadn't asked him to drop off the programs, he probably would have volunteered, knowing that Nadine would be here. He relished every chance to see her. He just wished that one day he could work up the nerve to tell Nadine how he'd truly felt about her all these years.

Nadine's furrowed eyebrows showed her suspicion because Denise hadn't mentioned missing rehearsal when they spoke two hours prior. Or maybe Denise had and Nadine was just too tired to remember. But had Nadine known in advance, she would have considered skipping rehearsal herself. She could barely stay awake. She glanced down at her watch, blinked sleepily.

Jeff tried not to stare at Nadine, but failed terribly. His disobedient eyes scanned her 5'8" frame. He was checking all of her out and with God as his witness, Nadine was still the finest woman he'd ever laid eyes on. "So where you heading off to?" he asked, examining her from a new angle.

Nadine's reply was uneven. "I'm headed home. It's so late." She stifled a yawn. "Excuse me. Not only is it past my bedtime, but your wife and I have an early meeting tomorrow with a client that wants us to analyze his accounts. Can you believe that after all the time we spent winning him over, he continues to make us jump through hoops and over hurdles to maintain just a piece of his portfolio?" She shook her head, allowing the frustration that had been lurking all day to show its ugly face. "All the money we made for him and now he's ready to bail out on us. Some people are so damn ungrateful—!" Nadine caught herself, raised her right hand to the sky, bit down on her tongue as a faint smile appeared. "Lord, forgive me. That was so unladylike."

Jeff shook his head, smiled. "Don't worry about it. You must have forgotten that I'm married to a woman that cusses like a sailor. Besides, if something is on your mind, let it off."

Nadine inhaled as much of the polluted night air as she could take in at once. "It's just"—she raised her hands and then dismissed the thought altogether once she felt herself getting worked up again—"Never mind."

Jeff stood directly in front of Nadine, taking in her radiant smile, sexy aura, and the beautiful personality that had first attracted him to her way back when. He often wondered what would have happened between them if he'd confessed to her early on that she was a longing desire he kept tucked in the nest of his heart. He imagined what it would have been like marrying Nadine instead of Denise. He envisioned Deandra, his daughter, having Nadine's brown, narrow eyes, round nose, and smooth butterscotch skin so enticing it was only a fraction away from appearing edible. And since the day they'd first met, he often fantasized about making love to Nadine whenever he was intimate with Denise. He imagined making memories between her legs as she counted backwards from ten, a digit for every inch of his blessings. He fantasized about stroking Nadine so deep that in the middle of her climax she'd call out his name in a cursing fit because he was fucking her so damn good. Then before she could even cross that finish line, he'd deepen his thrust, harden his stroke, grab her by the waist and force her warm erotic passion to surrender to his own as they rode the waves of ecstasy together. Jeff couldn't get Nadine out of his head and the only thing he felt guilty about was the realization he didn't want to. She supplied him with peace and didn't even know it.

"Oh! Have I lost my mind?" Nadine blurted, breaking Jeff's concentration with a smile that exposed straight white teeth shaped by childhood braces. "How could I stand here and not congratulate you on the new promotion? I hear you're running things now, Mr. General Manager." She straightened her posture. "So when I'm out of a job tomorrow," she said, pointing a perfectly manicured finger at herself and then at Jeff, "I'll be running over to your job. Sell a few cars, sweep some floors, hang balloons or something." She laughed. While Nadine was only joking, the weight of her last comment forced her to lean back against her driver door. It was as though she just set off an explosive the way the words ricocheted from her mouth, leaving a terrible aftertaste. The uncomfortable thought of working for anyone other than the extremely wealthy clients who bankrolled her lifestyle was depressing, not to mention a hard pill to swallow. She could never go back to the clock-punching days that barely financed a third of her wardrobe. She could barely eat off of those checks, she remembered painfully. If it hadn't been for the aunt that raised her and put her through school, she didn't know how she would have managed.

Before allowing the threat of losing their most prized client take hold of her, Nadine switched her mindset back to the present. She sucked in her lips. *Now what were we just talking about?* she thought. Finally remembering, she said, "So I guess everybody's *hustling* nowadays to maintain what they have. This recession has really hit us in the financial industry."

Listen to her. Jeff laughed inside at how she carefully pronounced every word. Even when Nadine tried to fit in and speak the lingo, the slang, it just didn't sound right coming out of her mouth. But her attempts were always flattering. "Yeah, everybody's gotta have a backup plan to stay on top of all this madness," he replied. "But speaking of hustling, Denise and I just got into an argument about that the other day. She thinks I'm working too much overtime, but hell, that was in my job description. She was unhappy with me *just* selling cars. Now that I'm managing the dealership, she's still unhappy."

Nadine's face showed her concern. Denise normally shared everything with Nadine about her marriage, but surprisingly she hadn't mentioned anything to Nadine about this. As far as Nadine knew, Denise was ecstatic about her husband being promoted to general manager; at least proud enough to share the news with the entire staff one day in a board meeting.

"Well, you guys will work it out," Nadine assured him with a questionable sincerity in her voice. She allowed herself a brief pause, then continued. "Seriously, how long have I known you two to go through these periods of being mad over nothing?" She answered for him, her neck moving with each word. "Too long. It must be a marriage thing," she said, shrugging her shoulders, at a loss for a better explanation. Before the sentence left her mouth though, Nadine knew she was lying to Jeff. She tried coaching herself on the next best thing to say until she saw the look of unhappiness swell in his eyes. What had she gotten herself into now? Jeff and Denise's marriage wasn't any business of hers, she kept telling herself, and it would only complicate things if she stood there and allowed him to express himself in a way that made Denise look like a foolish woman undeserving of a good man. Because that would open up doors. Doors she knew should remain closed.

The wind sent another invasive chill and, instantly, Nadine's nipples hardened into bullets as thick as her pinky. The swell of her breasts made the silver, buttoned-down blouse she wore dislodge itself from the waist of her pencil skirt. That should have been her cue to leave but instead she reached in her car, started the engine, and permitted the heat to circulate between them.

Jeff stared into thin air, then back at Nadine. "I just don't know sometimes." He tilted his head. "It's like whatever I do, it's just not good enough anymore," he exclaimed honestly. He couldn't figure out where he'd gone wrong in their relationship but it was apparent that Denise was so wrapped up in herself and everything else that he didn't even exist in her world. That was why it was so easy for him to put in fifty to eighty hours a week and not feel missed at home. When Denise did decide to throw the shit up in his face, it was right before they became intimate. But Jeff was no fool. He knew that it was just another lame ass excuse to keep him from bothering her for sex. So before the night was up, they would be screaming and shouting, then to the couch he would go to finish himself off alone. There was nothing about their marriage that felt special anymore; nothing that gave him a reason to come home every night or a reason to remain faithful. Everything leading up to the point he was at now had been a living hell. And while the pussy coupons women threw his way should have been the quick fix he needed, they did absolutely nothing for him. His only true interest was in one woman—Nadine Collins.

Nadine couldn't help but wonder where all Jeff's complaining was coming from. It was all so sudden, and not that she minded being a listening ear, tonight was just not a good night for it. She had no choice but to refuse to listen to his gripes about Denise, because she was already yawning and struggling to keep her eyes open, and also struggling to keep them from drifting down to the fly of his jeans. That may have actually been the bigger struggle. Oh how she wished just for one second that she had X-ray vision. She moved closer to him.

"Jeff, honey, I want you to try to relax," Nadine said in her calmest voice. She began rubbing his shoulders. He was tense, almost as tense as the muscles in her pussy. She focused on those stubborn knots, massaging her fingers deeply in and out of every groove. Before she knew it, she had gotten herself wet. She looked around the parking lot, which thankfully was now empty except for Jeff's black BMW parked in the far corner under a leaning thirty-foot elm tree. She didn't want to risk someone coming out of the church and seeing the two of them alone.

Jeff tried to loosen up under Nadine's irresistible touch. He didn't want her to feel sorry for him, or maybe he did. He wasn't sure what he wanted Nadine to feel. As long as he had her attention, he was content. "Nothing I do is good enough anymore," he went on to say. "All Denise does is nag. It's like she creates reasons to be pissed at me. And do you know how long it's been since we had sex? Y'all are girls so I know y'all talk about it." If Nadine didn't know, he was about to enlighten her. "Three months! She tell you that?" Jeff held up three stiff fingers. "Not one, not two, but three!"

Nadine stood wide-eyed and fully awake now. She had no idea all of this was happening, and right under her nose because Jeff was absolutely right; she talked to Denise about almost everything. No subject was off limits. At least that's how it used to be.

"Please, help me understand how a woman just loses the desire to be with her man," Jeff said. "Her husband." He stared at Nadine's face, studying her facial response like an open book test. "I mean, come on. Help a brother out. What is she thinking? Is she seeing somebody? You can tell me." He scratched at the coal black waves in his Caesar haircut. "I'm just not getting this shit right now."

Nadine didn't know what to do or say but she could both empathize and sympathize because she wasn't getting any loving either. She'd been celibate for what felt like a decade. Celibate after her last fling had given her crabs, had her rushing to the hospital like a damn fool for believing his two-timing ass when he told her he wasn't seeing anyone else. Since then she vowed to refrain from sex until the timing was right. She'd been so engulfed in work lately she hadn't had the time or patience to date. Besides, in her book, most men were dogs and she refused to waste the time and energy searching for Mr. Right when she had Mr. Right Quick tucked away safely in her bedside nightstand.

"Jeff, I think you really need to talk to your wife about all this. I mean"—Nadine's eyes widened as she flipped both her hands over—"don't you think Denise is the one that needs to hear everything that you're telling *me?*" She hoped she wasn't being hypocritical by saying so.

"Nadine, Denise and I have had the talk a thousand times. It's come to the point where it's pointless with her. She ain't hearing me." He sounded like a man out on his last limb. Speaking with no certainty, hope, or faith for a future with Denise as husband and wife. He could feel the wrinkles in his forehead beginning to form naturally like they've done throughout the course of his marriage. He often wondered if they were permanent lines of love, hate, and unhappiness that would one day interfere with the man whom he had set out to be.

"Maybe I'm just asking for too much. I bet that's it. Where is the woman that doesn't mind if her man is the main breadwinner, the head of the household, the father to their children, and her lover when it's time to be?" Jeff shook his head and took a deep breath. "I guess it's silly of me to think such a woman exists. Hell, I shouldn't have to be in competition with my wife!"

Jeff's titanium wedding band shone like a knight's armor even in the darkest hour. This symbolic piece of jewelry made its statement so loud and clear that Nadine had to avert her eyes. She forced back a silent jealousy that nearly washed up the day's dinner; now a little apprehensive about carrying on the rest of their conversation. Her ears drew themselves to the sound the leaves made as they rustled across the pavement. Maybe the leaves' efforts to escape from their original habitat was Nadine's second cue to get the hell up out of here herself. But while there were so many reasons she needed to turn around and leave, there was only one that kept her standing on her feet with her heated pussy inviting itself into their conversation.

"Jeff, I really wish I could stay and talk about this with you, but, I don't think I'm the most suitable person to give you relationship advice. I don't even have a man myself." She smiled, hoping the gesture would save her from continuing the chat. She didn't feel it was appropriate to discuss Denise's bedroom drama with Jeff. Something about it didn't sit well, but she couldn't deny that being in Jeff's company felt so damn good. His conversation made her moist. Tempted her in ways she didn't realize she could be tempted. Mind-fucked her thoughts so deeply she was on the verge of having a mental climax, if that were even possible.

Nadine snatched her mind out of the gutter. They were just talking. No harm in just talking, she told herself. She begged for the right words to come but they were somewhere resting in the cracks of her mental palace. They'd locked themselves up and ingested the keys. "What I mean is," she continued, "or I can only assume, that men and women go through periods where they stop..." She was silenced before she could complete her sentence. Jeff leaned in, halting her with a kiss so passionate and so intense. She lifted her hands in the air, trying with little success to avoid touching his body. Fearful that once in his embrace she wouldn't be able to let go. She began pulling away. "Jeff!" She quickly wiped her mouth, looking behind Jeff for a moving soul. From what she could see the coast was still clear.

2

Jeff backed away slowly, shocked by his own actions more than anything. He took a look around. They were on God's property. He felt guilty a hundred times over. Swore he heard the flames of Hell whistling his name. "Nadine, I'm so sorry," he tried apologizing. "I shouldn't—" He shook his head in disgust before stopping altogether, trying to find at least an ounce of composure while leaving his apology incomplete. "Please, Nadine, Denise doesn't have to know what happened here tonight."

That quickly Nadine had almost forgotten who Denise was. She pulled her long stream of extensions to the right side of her face. A pregnant pause juggled the words that went unsaid. "I won't say anything," she rattled out. "We just can't ever let it happen again." Nadine sucked in her lip, sampling the sweetness Jeff had left on her mouth to savor long after he was gone. A part of her couldn't resist the excitement she felt. She pulled nervously at her blouse, wishing she could rip the damn thing clean off and reveal the buttercups in Victoria's Secret made to look like full moons on a dark and chilly December night. But instead, she fanned herself as if the breeze blowing over her shoulders wasn't cool enough. Every thought was without purpose at that moment because all that she was capable of really considering was how she wanted to feel Jeff again.

"Well, I guess I better get my ass on home," Jeff stated through the sudden awkwardness that engulfed them. "I've caused enough trouble for one night." He was too embarrassed to look at Nadine's face now. He could only guess all the things she must have been thinking of him.

Nadine moved forward, slowly, closer to Jeff's hard body. She refused to let him leave her this way. In this predicament. Fuck her disagreeing good-girl conscience. She placed her lips on his again and, using her hands, gradually began making a long overdue love connection. Her fingers crawled underneath Jeff's shirt, up his solid six-pack, and over the fine black hairs spread across his chest. She inhaled his masculinity, falling in love with the scent of a man she'd only dreamed of being this close to. Her hands moved upward, allowing her fingers to snake his neck, his goatee, and the trim of his mustache.

Jeff stood there motionless, refusing to stop her. He wanted what Nadine wanted, probably more so than she.

Even in her four-inch Casadei pumps, Nadine's head only reached Jeff's shoulders. She fastidiously unbuckled his belt, unzipped his jeans, and blindly reached in through the opening. She let out a stricken gasp as her fingers traveled up and down the trunk of his dick. His pubic hairs prickled her skin as he grew in the palm of her hand. Each and every artery her fingers rolled over had a heartbeat of its own.

"Oh my God," Nadine said, panting, reacting to how well endowed he was. She stroked him to a silent satisfaction, feeling his dick stretch all of its ten full inches. This was torture, but that didn't stop her at all. She wanted Jeff so damn bad that her taste buds were sweating.

Jeff dropped the church programs he'd been holding in his hand. They landed at his feet. He tangled his fingers in Nadine's hair, drowning himself in the soft floral scent that oozed from her pores. Two tiny steps backwards and he was up against her car, fighting a losing battle. He gave into the temptation as she handled him below. A stronger breeze blew right over them and violated his manhood the second his pants hit the ground. He watched Nadine's beautiful face gradually disappear until the only visual that remained of her was the top of her head. He nearly lost it when her mouth began to caress his dick, leaving him overwhelmed with newborn fantasies. "Not here. Not like this," he murmured, unable to contain himself.

Nadine used the head of his penis to trace all the features on her face, starting with her nose, her shapely thin cocoa-painted lips, and her slight doubled chin. Excitement leaked from his tip and if there were any doubts, they'd faded away. He was enjoying this as much as Nadine was. She examined his manhood one final time, thinking of the favoritism the Creator showed when He made Jeff. She eased out her tongue, curved it a little, then allowed the syrupy glaze that coated the head of his shaft to lube her throat.

"Aww shit," Jeff cried out. He couldn't watch, not even for a second. So as his dick fell into the warm oven of Nadine's mouth, he fought to not let go and make himself out to be an embarrassment. It'd been so long. So long since he'd felt a feeling as great as the one he was experiencing at that moment. He was unstable and almost at the brink of sending his children down the back of her throat when she stopped suddenly. He opened his eyes, fearing that something was wrong.

Nadine swallowed the appetizing marinade that coated the inside of her mouth. Jeff's hands were already traveling over her body, befriending her small breasts every chance they got. With her lips still wrapped around his head, she bottled as much of him as she could fit into her mouth, moaning with anticipation. Just when Jeff thought Nadine was done, she picked up her pace, sending him back on a thrill ride down her esophagus.

The way Nadine deep-throated him, Jeff worried he'd rip out her tonsils. He let her have her way with him. This was her ball, her court. He was only a visitor, thankful enough for the playtime. "You're taking me there," he warned her. "I can't...control what happens." He had to talk his nut down to keep from exploding.

Nadine allowed Jeff to slide from between her lips as she stood readily to her feet. His mouth moved up her slim neck, planting tight kisses along the way. She was so tasty not even his wife could substitute for a taste as fulfilling.

"Fuck me. Here. Now," Nadine whined in his ear. She was so caught up in the moment that she refused to be taken lightly. She was hot, her pussy was begging for his yardage, and she needed comfort. She wanted to be sure he knew just that. She held him tightly as his head moved between her shirt, his teeth yanking off the nickel-sized buttons on her $200 blouse along the way. "Oh yes!" she squealed in delight. She held on like a horseback rider, propping one leg on the driver's seat as he tickled her nipples with his tongue. His head started to move further below and suddenly she felt a cold chill sneak up her spine. Jeff was sliding up her skirt, leaving the responsibility of keeping her warm completely to the heater as he tasted the flesh between her pasty thighs. Before she knew it, before she could get a hold of herself, his tongue was sliding up against the thin lace outlining her thong. "Oh Jeff!" she moaned.

Jeff lifted Nadine from her feet and maneuvered her body into the car. He eased her across the beige leather seats, sending everything on the passenger side flying to the floor. With the tail of her skirt hiked way above her stomach, Nadine's underwear was the only thing keeping him from going after what he longed for. Being the determined man that he was when it came down to moments like this, he slid those cock-blockers to the side. Her freshly waxed middle greeted him as her glistening lips encouraged his dick to reconsider its position, but Jeff's tongue argued for the first sampling.

Nadine spread her legs as far apart as the tight space they were in would allow. She looked up, watching the twinkling stars through her sunroof. It all seemed surreal. She took a deep breath and felt her skin break out in chills once Jeff's lips brushed against her hairless pussy in a swift upward motion. They enveloped her so tightly.

Hungry for it, his tongue dived between her drunken lips for the third and fourth time. Nadine began to experience her nut awakening from its coma. She matched his movements, ready to be taken there.

Jeff pleased Nadine orally with dinner table manners. He wanted every ounce of what she offered and he didn't dare stop. But his dick was weighing him down, knocking him off balance. Something had to give.

When Nadine felt just the mushroom top of Jeff's hardness rise up inside of her, she knew she hadn't felt a damn thing yet. She tried to brace herself, pulling at his jacket until she heard it rip in two places.

He plunged into Nadine in short, then deeper strokes. Each thrust taking his mind further and further away from his wife and the unhappily married category of which he was a member...